Broken

KING

Green Hills Academy Trilogy
Book 3

Josie Max

BROKEN KING

Copyright © 2021 by Josie Max.

For information contact :
Josie Max at josiemax@josiemaxwrites.com
http://www.josiemaxwrites.com

Cover design by Josie Max
ISBN: 978-1-955184-02-1

First Edition: March 2021

978-1-955184-02-1

CONTENTS

BROKEN KING

PROLOGUE

Violet

THE SLIP INTO SORROW was abrupt. Like crossing the street without looking both ways, and suddenly, I was hit with something that snuffed out my breath in an instant.

That was how I felt stepping into my home. The trailer.

But was it mine anymore? I knew it wouldn't be long before the landlord asked for rent. Money I didn't have.

My lip trembled as I scanned the room, just as I remembered it last night before I went to bed. I had my mother's tea after our fight, an argument I could barely remember now—not that I wanted to.

"We don't have to do this now. How about we wait a few days? Then we can come back and get your things." Aunt Dahlia's voice was warm, and her hand comforting as it rested on my shoulder.

"No. I need to find it." My voice was barely a whisper.

My mother hadn't even been dead a day. Memories of the police pulling her body out of that pond flashed behind my eyes at the most random moments. Like earlier, when I was eating lunch, or now, as I scanned the room for a note.

A suicide note.

"Violet." Dahlia stepped in front of me as her green eyes locked onto mine. "It's too soon. I think this is something for another day. Being here is only going to make you feel worse when you should work on taking care of yourself. You're still in shock, honey. Let's head back to my place. You can sleep in my bed until I make up the spare bedroom. Okay?"

It wasn't okay.

I felt the rage bubble up. Not at my aunt but at my mom. She fucking left me. I wasn't even eighteen yet and still had over a year until I graduated high school. If her life was so damn horrible that she had to leave it immediately and drag my sleeping body with her so I had a horrifying wake-up call, she could have at least waited until I was an adult. Until I could go out into the world and fend for myself.

No, as usual, she only thought about herself.

"I just . . ." I took a fortifying breath before I did something stupid like raise my voice to the most loving aunt a girl could wish for. "Can you give me five minutes? Alone. Wait in the car if you want, but I really need this. For my sanity."

She scanned my face. Her eyes flickered around like a curious bird. I held my breath, my heart beating so fast I worried it might explode. I wished it would. Then the nightmare would be over. I wouldn't have to deal with my mom's suicide.

"Okay. Take as much time as you need. And here, "she reached into the pocket of her trench coat, "here are some tissues. Just in case."

Dahlia gave a sad smile, pushing the small pack of tissues into my hand. It crinkled in my fingers as I tightened my grip around the offering.

I watched her leave, and when the door closed, my feet stomped on the floor until I flopped headfirst onto the sofa. Inhaling, I caught a whiff of my mom's perfume, and it hit me hard. My mouth pushed open as if I were about to scream, but nothing came out. My body tightened until I was tucked into a ball as the silent sob overwhelmed me.

She was gone. My mom wasn't perfect. Her life was a wild ride of highs and lows as she navigated addiction. Some years were filled with stability, while others were like living with a zombie—a very emotional and volatile zombie.

Time slipped past without a care from

me as I sobbed, clinging to a pillow I knew my mom always propped her head on when she lay on the couch. My fingers gripped it like it could grow arms and hug me back.

Why had she done it? That thought kept wiggling in the back of my head. No matter how much I swatted the question away, it always buzzed in my ear.

"I thought you were happy. I thought you loved me." My voice was raw. I scrunched up my face as a fresh wave of tears flowed.

"Fuck you, Mom!" I screamed. "Fuck you for leaving me."

I sat up. I felt an instant boost of energy as anger took over for despair. I liked anger; it got me up and made me think. I was an active participant in my life with resentment holding my hand.

It was time to find that note. Anything

that gave a sign as to why she died.

The trailer wasn't big, so it didn't take long for me to rummage through every cabinet, drawer, and box. I even checked in the toilet tank. Not that I thought anything out of the ordinary would be in there, but I was desperate.

I learned something today. Mom had little, even less than I did. Few clothes, no jewelry. The only pictures she had of me were when I was a baby and one when I was ten at a park on the north side. A few people were in the background as I stood there pretending to smell a flower. She even had me wear a dress as if it were a special occasion. It wasn't, just a random warm spring afternoon.

I shrugged and placed the pictures on the kitchen counter, intending to take them with me. With one last glance around the dingy trailer, I was ready to grab the pictures and go.

But a thought stopped me in my tracks. *My hiding spot in the woods . . .* It was the one place only my mom and I knew about.

When I was five, she went on a bender, leaving me alone overnight. I created it the next morning. When my aunt found out, she was angry and threatened to take me away.

I created a spot in the woods. I was young and thought my mom was just lost, and that was why she never came home. I told her if she couldn't find her way home again to leave me a note there.

She told me I was smart to come up with such a clever plan. She left notes for me there over the years. It was the one place where our love for each other couldn't be tainted.

I pushed open the trailer door and ran around it toward the woods. Despite my lack of sleep and my emotions beating the crap out of me today, I ran as if I were in a race, hopping over fallen trees and letting vines lash my face without caring if I was bleeding.

I fell to my knees when I came to the tree marked with a flower carved into the bark. I gasped for air as the effects of dashing to the spot sank in. I didn't care that I was out of breath; I pushed the dead leaves away and dug into the soft soil until I found the box. An old burnt-orange Tupperware lid popped against the dark brown dirt. Once I could slip my fingers under the rim, I pulled the container out. I peeled back the lid after a quick shake to get rid of the excess soil.

I hadn't realized I was smiling until it slowly slipped away. There was something in the box, but it wasn't a note. Just a cheap metal charm bracelet that my mom gave me for my sixteenth birthday. The fake jeweled charms twinkled as I lifted it from the box.

I didn't remember placing it there, but maybe I had.

"Who fucking cares about this crappy bracelet? And why does it have a tiny key on it? Was that some kind of symbol, Mom? A key to your heart? You don't have a heart. Because if you did, you wouldn't have killed yourself." My voice rose higher with each word until my throat burned from my screaming.

I threw the bracelet hard and saw it hit the tree where I had once innocently carved a flower. A violet.

My dirt-stained fingers curled into my hair as I cried. I knew what that meant. There was no note.

It meant that whatever we fought about had hurt her so much that she'd rather die than live with me anymore. I did this to her. I caused my mom to walk into that cold pond and never walk back out.

That was why she brought me there with her. So when I woke up, I'd be the first to glimpse what I had done to her.

"It's all my fault," I repeated as I rocked myself on the cold, damp forest floor.

"No, it's not."

I gasped and lifted my head at the sound of my aunt's voice. She stood there looking down at me.

"It is. Why else would she do this?"

She sighed and lowered herself to the ground beside me. "Your mom died of a broken heart, honey. I didn't want to admit it, but she's been battling that hurt for so long. She loved your father so much."

Dahlia bit her bottom lip and turned her head. It took a few moments, but she cleared her throat and continued, "I was so wrong to pull them apart, but I thought he was using her. She refused to tell me his name, only that he was wealthy. Then when she became pregnant and he disappeared, it only solidified my resentment of him. I guess I used my experience with men as the basis for all men. I was wrong to do that, and I have regretted it every day of your life."

I placed my hand on her shoulder. "Don't blame yourself. If my father wanted to be in my life, he would have found a way."

She opened her mouth to say something but shook her head instead. Dahlia got up and brushed off her hands. Taking a few steps, she reached down and picked up the bracelet.

"Your, uh . . . mom wanted you to have this. You have little from her to hold on to, but you have this."

I hopped up, brushing the dirt off my jeans.

"Here," she said and placed it in my hand.

"It is pretty, even if it's cheap." I slipped it on and turned my wrist, watching it sparkle.

Dahlia threw her arm over my shoulder. "Why don't we go back to my place, huh? I can make you some hot chocolate, and we can watch a movie."

"How about *Moana*? I need to be somewhere far away and tropical right now." We began to walk away from my spot and left the Tupperware exposed to the elements. There was no point putting it back anymore.

"Sounds like heaven." She gave me a squeeze as we left the woods.

My fingers twisted the little gold key that hung from the bracelet as we made our way back to the car. Maybe my aunt was right. I hadn't felt better in my old home. It was too much of a reminder of what I had lost.

It was time to leave for good.

ONE

Knight

Seven Months Later

I WAVED BACK AT Edwin as I left his home—he had moved a few towns away for his family's safety. I glanced around the street and noticed a man I had hired sitting in a car parked in sight of the house.

Good.

He was safe, for now.

I was relieved, but even more, I was interested in what he had given me. We didn't talk about anything of interest in case someone had bugged his home. I gave him a bug sweeper like the one I had.

But he had given me a note, along with a large folder.

I let out a breath once I was in my car. It had been a long two years. And I knew what I held in my hand might help bring my uncle down.

Finally.

I knew he played a role in my parents' death and was wondering if he also killed Violet's mom.

Placing the folder on the passenger seat, I unfolded the note Edwin wrote.

My eyes widened as I read:

There were three key investors in the failed cancer drug. Ichabod King, Kiki King, and

Crystal Hillingham. I discovered that the drug was now being used illegally. Not to help with cancer, but as a recreational drug. It causes an intense high and is extremely addictive.

That was why they invested so much into a failed drug. It was extremely profitable.

I set the note aside and was about to pick up the folder to view its contents when a thought entered my head.

Violet is with Crystal at her luncheon.

If my uncle wanted something from Violet, then Crystal knew what that thing was.

Violet might be in more danger than I thought.

I reached into my jacket pocket and pulled out my phone. After a few taps, I opened the app that kept track of Violet.

The necklace with the flower pendant I gave Violet—the one that was my mom's—

served two purposes. One was that I wanted her to have it. It was a beautiful piece of jewelry, and Violet deserved something that made her smile.

The other purpose was why I placed a tracking device on it. I thought my uncle would try to get to her at the luncheon, but I never suspected Mrs. Hillingham would be the one I needed to worry about.

Once the app was open, I noticed I had lost the signal. I rubbed my neck. She should have plenty of signal connection in that house.

Something was wrong.

Tapping at the recording feature of the app, I played the previous fifteen minutes before the app lost connection.

I heard Crystal tell Violet to help her by getting a box of dishes from the basement. I smiled when I heard her call herself a work of art. She was gorgeous, and that dress looked amazing on her.

There was some noise, and then it cut out. The sound went in and out. Suddenly, I heard banging and Violet yelling that the door was locked.

Iciness gripped me when I heard Seraphina.

"Oh my god. Crystal wanted Violet locked in the basement," I muttered.

I continued to listen and was shocked by how much Seraphina admitted to Violet. She talked about her mom's friend making money off Jack Franklin's failed drug. That must have been what Edwin was telling me about—the investment Crystal made.

The only other people who invested were my uncle and Kiki. I doubted Kiki was smart enough to come up with the idea herself, so it must've been my uncle.

But why did Seraphina tell Violet she

was in the way? What would Violet have to do with Jack Franklin's failed drug?

The sound cut out. I threw the phone into the driver's seat and raced back to town. I was about a half an hour away, so I called Briggs.

"What do you want?" he asked, still upset with me.

"I bailed Edwin out of jail. I just came from his house and have protection on him."

There was silence.

"Briggs. You there?"

"Yeah. Thanks for helping him."

I sighed. I missed him. Spending the past week not speaking made me realize my friends were more important than helping me get my uncle; they were my family.

"I was an ass. I fucked up. Thanks for being a friend and telling me how it is."

"Anytime, Knight. What are up to?"

"Just heading to the police station."

"Please tell me I'm not your one call. What did you do to get yourself locked up?"

I chuckled. "No, man. I'm driving in my car. I think Mrs. Hillingham and Seraphina have kidnapped Violet. I have a recording I think the police are going to be very interested in. Meet me there. Oh, and call Caleb too."

"Oh shit. I'm going to head out."

"Thanks. I'll meet you there."

I ended the call and pressed on the gas once I was on the highway. After what felt like hours—but was only twenty minutes after I spoke to Briggs—I was finally at the police station.

Briggs and Caleb were waiting on a bench inside the precinct.

"Dude, this is so fucked up," Caleb said

as he hopped up and followed me toward one of the officer's desks.

"Excuse me, Officer. Can you help me? I believe someone has kidnapped my girlfriend." I held my phone in my hand, ready to play the recording.

The woman looked up. It was the same one who had arrested Violet a month ago.

"Kidnapped? How long has she been missing?"

"Only about two hours, but—"

"Two hours? I'm sorry, young man, but she's not missing. She's just not answering your calls," she said with a snort.

"Here, just listen." I held out my phone and played the recording.

Her eyes widened the more she heard.

Once it ended, she asked, "Who is your girlfriend?" She lifted a pad of paper and a pencil, ready to get all the information I could give her.

"Her name is Violet Adler. And the other girl's voice you heard, the one threatening her, is Seraphina Hillingham."

The woman stopped writing and glanced up at me. "Hillingham. Ugh . . ." She glanced around, clearly nervous.

"This was at the Hillingham home," I added when she didn't continue.

She stood so suddenly that her chair bumped into her trash can, knocking it over. She reached down and picked up the old paper coffee cups that had fallen out.

"I wish I could help you, but until someone is officially missing for at least twenty-four hours—"

"That's not true." Briggs stepped forward, folding his arms over his chest. "That's a myth, and you know it."

The woman coughed and garbled out a few "uhs" and "mmms."

"Why don't I walk you boys out?" She

raised her brows while staring at me.

She tried to place her hand on my shoulder to guide me toward the door, but I pulled back. "No. She's in trouble and needs help."

The officer glanced around the station with weary eyes. A few people stopped what they were doing and gazed over at me.

"And that's what I plan to do," she bit out through her teeth. "Now, please, come outside."

Caleb tugged at my jacket and tilted his head toward the door. I wasn't sure what was going on, but I nodded.

"Fine. But just know that if anything happens to Violet, I don't think the local department will be all too happy when their yearly officer's ball takes place in the bowling alley instead of the King home."

It was something my parents did every

year for the past decade. Once they died, my uncle was smart enough to keep holding the annual fundraiser at my home.

"Noted. Now come with me."

She led the way, but once we were outside, she kept walking until we were a block away and had turned a corner. Finally, she stopped in front of Pop's Dry Cleaners.

"There's a reason I couldn't say anything inside the station." She glanced around before leaning toward me. "Your uncle is friends with the chief. And the chief is friends with a few of the officers . . . if you know what I mean."

I swallowed. I knew exactly what she meant. My uncle made sure he had a few members of the police force on his side. And I wouldn't be surprised if several of them did his bidding.

Briggs took a step forward. "But why would rescuing Violet from the Hillingham's home have anything to do with that?"

"A few weeks ago, an officer started nosing around the bus accident that happened near Winter River University. Now he's on vacation, and no one knows where he is. We haven't heard from him in a week . . . and neither has his wife. But the chief keeps assuring us that everything is fine. That was a Hillingham bus. When something happens to one of our own, we jump on it fast. But the chief is acting like it's nothing."

I knew something was wrong with that bus accident, but I had no idea it was so bad.

"But Mr. Hillingham did his own investigation. He found out it was faulty parts and is now replacing them in all his buses."

The officer swallowed and shook her head. "It wasn't faulty anything. Here's what I know." She glanced around again, clearly nervous. "The officer who went missing is a friend. He told me there were parts that had been cut out with something sharp. Clean cuts. Wear and tear doesn't do that. Someone tampered with it."

"Seraphina mentioned Violet had nine lives. She must have been referring to the bus accident. Either Seraphina or her mom did it," I said.

"It must be her mom. Do you think Seraphina is smart enough to know which wires to cut to cause the brakes to fail?" Briggs added.

"Or to purposely get dirty trying to make it happen by fiddling under the bus's hood?" Caleb pointed out.

"You're both right." I rubbed my chin.

"Thanks for the inside information, but that doesn't help me get my girlfriend out of there."

She placed her hand on my shoulder. "Look, I get that you care for her, and I wish there was something I could do . . .. But you might as well be asking me to break into the White House. I can tell you there's a journalist who's been keeping tabs on your uncle for a few years. Her name is Georgia Ellis." She reached into her pocket and pulled out a small business card, then placed it in my hand. "Here's her card. Reach out to her; I know she'd want to hear from you."

"I'm sorry I can't do more. I remember Violet. She's a nice girl stuck in the middle of a terrible situation. If a cop even showed up at the Hillingham's just as a courtesy call, the chief would find out, and then one of us might disappear too." She patted me on the shoulder and then turned, heading back to the police department.

"Shit. What do we do now?" Briggs asked.

I glanced up at the guys and smiled. "We crash the party."

TWO

Violet

MY ASS CHEEKS WERE numb from sitting on the floor for so long. My fingers gripped the edge of the photograph of my mom and dad as if it might disappear at any moment.

I stared at him. No matter how much I squinted, I couldn't make out his eye color. My mom said he had brown eyes, just like me. She had always described my eyes as a rich caramel color. I suspected it was to make me feel better for not having her eye color. I used to complain when I was little that my eye color was an ugly brown, which was when she called it caramel.

Given my love of sweets, I accepted it as the best thing ever. Now I wondered if she had first said it to him. Did she tell my dad she loved his caramel-colored eyes?

"I can hardly believe that Jack Franklin is my dad. It had to be the same Jack Franklin who died in the plane crash with Knight's parents," I said to myself for the hundredth time.

I had no clue how much time had passed since being trapped in the Hillingham's basement. With no reception on my phone, it read 12:20. It had been like that for a while. When I sat near the door, a bar of signal would occasionally appear on my phone. But right as I opened the phone app, it would disappear.

I finally shut it off. I didn't want to drain the battery in case I got a chance and escaped the room. But as each minute flickered by, sorrow replaced the little hope I had left.

My mom had a horrible death, as did my dad. I guess it was my fate too. Maybe it was a family curse or just really shitty luck.

"Stop feeling sorry for yourself, Violet." I did my best to snap out of it.

I stood and shook my hands. Lifting my arms overhead, I stretched. It was time for a plan—and a backup plan in case the first one failed. I was an Adler—we were strong and wouldn't go down without a fight.

Scanning the room, I went back over every box I had ransacked. Perhaps I missed something, anything that would help get the door open.

My mind drifted to Knight as I got down on my knees and searched through the boxes. *I wish Knight were here . . ..* He'd be able to pick the lock.

Seraphina and her mom were liars and, if I died in their basement, murderers. But Seraphina was on to something when she questioned why Knight was at Happy Pond the night my mom died.

And now that I knew I was Jack Franklin's daughter, it made more sense that she was killed. My mother told me it was more complicated than I thought when I asked why he couldn't be with us. She mentioned there were people who wouldn't want me around.

Having lived on the north side for two months, I understood what she meant. Mrs. Hillingham tried to kill me, and her daughter happily did her bidding. Knight's uncle wanted to gang rape me. It was no wonder my mom kept my father a secret from me.

Fresh tears rolled down my face, and I pushed the half-emptied box aside. "I'm sorry, Mom. I was such a selfish asshole. You worked so hard to protect me, and I hated you for it."

A sob shook my body. It felt freeing to admit it, if only to myself. I loved my mom, but there were times I hated her too. I never understood why we struggled. Why she couldn't just stop using and tell me about my dad?

Since I met Knight and Jewel and all the people during the year, I realized the tightrope my mom walked everyday just to keep us safe. The stress of it all must have driven her to drugs.

All that greed destroyed so many lives.

I wiped my cheeks on my sleeve. Looking down, I frowned. The beautiful dress was ruined, covered in dirt, tears, and mascara.

I lifted the jeweled flower pendant that hung down my chest. "At least you're still beautiful."

Flipping it over, I saw it was set in gold, but in the middle was something black and plastic.

"What the hell . . .?"

How had I not noticed that before? I guessed I was too dazzled by the jewels to turn it over.

I picked at the black thing until it fell off. I had an idea what it was but wanted a closer look. I went to lift it up, but then I heard some noise come from the basement.

Scurrying over to the door, I pressed my ear against it. The voices were deep, definitely not Seraphina or her mom.

I banged as hard as I could and screamed, "Help!"

There was no stopping me. My voice was hoarse, but I kept it up. My hand ached and arm burned, but I wouldn't stop.

"Violet?" a familiar voice came through the door.

"Briggs. Oh, thank God! I'm locked in here."

"She's here." I heard him call out.

Soon there were other voices, one of which was Knight.

"Violet. Don't worry. We'll get you out."

My shoulders sagged with sweet relief that I wouldn't die alone. That the family curse of terrible deaths wouldn't befall me, at least not today.

"Caleb, go set it up. Just in case," Knight said.

"What? Set what up? Should I move from the door?" I asked, uncertain if what they were setting up involved explosives.

When it came to Knight, I had no idea what to expect.

"Unnecessary. Just a security measure in case someone discovers us down here," he said.

"You broke in?"

"Yes," Briggs answered.

"You say 'broke in,' but I say we came to rescue you. Which sounds better?" Knight asked.

"It doesn't matter which sounds better. It's what holds up in court if they catch us that matters," Briggs added.

If they went to jail for breaking me out, I'd sell plasma to help pay for a lawyer—

not that they needed help with money.

"They kidnapped her. I don't care what it sounds like. Besides, there's no way Mrs. Hillingham is going to touch me," Knight said.

"I wouldn't be so sure of that." Crystal's voice came from farther away.

It was muffled, and I had to press my ear to the door to hear her.

"You will not get away with this. You can't just kidnap people," Knight said.

"I think this gun would say differently."

I gasped. She had a gun, and even if I couldn't see them, I was sure it was pointed at the guys.

"No," I cried out and banged on the door.

"Aren't you dead yet? I thought I told Seraphina to give you that smoothie."

"What smoothie? She slammed the door shut, and I had no idea it was her until she said something."

"Damn that stupid girl. She was supposed to give you the smoothie, then shut the door and lock it. You'd die much quicker that way. Now you'll just go more slowly from dehydration and starvation. I guess my daughter wanted you to suffer."

What the fuck? That entire family was messed up.

"You're fucking sick," Briggs said.

"No, dear, I'm fucking wealthy. And to stay wealthy, people sometimes have to do messed-up things . . . Well, it's survival of the fittest. And, unfortunately, Violet wasn't fit. She has to go."

"No, she doesn't. Just let us all go, and we won't say a word."

Crystal laughed. "You two are funny."

Two? Was Caleb not there? My heart pounded in my chest. Maybe he went to get help. That must be what Knight was telling Caleb to do. Maybe set up a call with the police?

"Hilarious," Knight deadpanned.

"I find it fascinating that we both come from the same trailer park, yet only one of us could hack it here. I survived, but Violet will die. And since my daughter has trouble doing as she's told, I'll just have to shoot Violet. Do it quick, in the head, just like I did that, well, never mind about that."

"So you've killed before?" Knight asked.

"Let's just say there was someone who got in the way of plans. I like to help my friends," Crystal said with an evil curl to her lips.

"It seems your friends want you to be a serial killer." Knight waved his hands between us.

"Shut up. You're one to talk. Seraphina

told me how you tampered with Ichabod's food."

"It was only to make him sick. He's an asshole and deserved every second he hugged the porcelain god. You know as much as I do that I was being lenient."

"Yeah, well, if you must know . . . I told Ichabod that you tried to kill him. I thought it best he know that his nephew wanted to hurt him."

There was silence, and I wished I could see what was happening. I glanced around for anything to get me out, but it was futile. I would have found something by now; nothing new was about to suddenly appear.

I groaned and pounded my fist against the door.

"Pound all you want, Violet. You and your friends don't have much longer. In fact, why don't you boys join her?"

I heard some feet shuffling and then a ding sound, like metal hitting a hard surface.

"Take that key and open the door. I got the gun pointed right at you, so I wouldn't try anything funny. I've spent many years practicing at a gun range, so it would be unwise to think I don't know what I'm doing."

I ran over to a box of broken plates. I had thought earlier that I could use the broken china to pick the lock, but it didn't work. If I could get close enough to Crystal, I could hold it to her neck and get her to drop her gun.

She might have known how to shoot, but I knew how to pin someone in a hold they couldn't get out of—one of the many things I had picked up from the south side.

I picked up a few pieces of jagged china and hid my hands behind my back.

The door popped open, and a smile grew as my eyes landed on Knight. He ran over and slipped his arms around me. As he did that, I pushed a piece of broken plate into his hand. He pulled back and quickly examined what I gave him before slipping it in his back pocket and turning to face the door. Briggs stared at me warily as I went up to him, grabbing his hand and placing a piece in his hand.

"Briggs, thank God you're okay."

His eyes widened when he realized what I had done.

"I should say that to you." He winked at me before he turned to face our killer.

"What a lovely reunion, but I'm afraid I can't stay long. Got a luncheon to attend to, and the guests should be arriving any minute. Don't worry, though, I'll make this quick. I'm not vengeful like my daughter. Three shots, and it will be done." Crystal stood in the doorway with the gun pointed right at us.

She did something to the gun that made it click. I assumed it was the safety, but I had never fired a gun in my life. All I knew was that if the safety was off, it wasn't good.

My mind raced, and it felt like time slowed as I tried to figure out how to stop her. If I ran and tackled her, I would get shot, but the guys would be saved.

Knight put his arm around me and pulled me behind his body. I tried to push away from his grip, but it was firm. It was too late. We were all about to die.

THREE

Violet

A TEAR FELL FROM my eye. Thoughts of my mom, my aunt, the father I never knew, and even little Ava filled my head.

My aunt lost her sister earlier this year, and now she would lose her niece. And

Ava would lose the only family she had left.

Anger welled up inside me. It was intense and like nothing I had felt before—even stronger than when the mayor tried to rape me.

"No, you fucking don't!" I screamed and pushed Knight away.

Crystal's eyes grew in surprise, but the shock didn't last. A smile curved her lips as she said, "I'm the one with the gun, honey. I most certainly do."

Her arm lifted, and right at that moment, I saw movement behind her. Someone with blond hair. Maybe it was the rage blinding me, but I thought it was Seraphina coming to help Mommy Dearest.

I was wrong. There was a loud thud, and something cracked. Crystal's eyes fluttered, and within seconds, she was falling.

She collapsed into a heap on the ground, the gun hitting the floor with a crack, sliding right over to Knight's feet.

I looked up. It was Caleb, and he held a large framed mirror in his hand. The corner dripped with blood, and I realized it was the mirror I had admired my reflection in when I came down to the basement.

"Are you guys okay?" he asked, holding the mirror as if Crystal might get up any second.

"Fine. Thanks, man. I thought for sure this was the end, and I was so pissed at Knight." Briggs slid his gaze to Knight.

"Hey, I was kind of pissed at myself too. I should have brought a weapon." He tossed the broken china plate aside.

"At least Violet was thinking." Briggs held up his piece of the plate. "Thanks."

"I had no idea how we would use it, but if the opportunity rose, we each had something we could use."

"Are we done slapping each other on the back? Because we have to do something about this." Caleb pointed at the heap of Crystal on the floor.

Knight reached down to touch her neck. "She's only knocked out, not dead."

"I say we lock her in here." My nose flared as I glared at Mrs. Hillingham.

"Sounds like a plan. But then what? We can't go to the police." Briggs' eyes darted between all of us.

I shoved my hands on my hips. "Why not?"

Knight's shoulders slumped. "Briggs is right. We tried to go to the police before we came here, but my uncle has the cops paid off, even the chief. I'm at a loss."

We stared at Knight. He always had a

plan and knew what to do. Even after the mayor tried to rape me, I felt some comfort knowing Knight was looking out for me. But if he didn't know what to do, we were all lost.

"I'll contact my parents," Caleb said in a low voice.

"No," Knight said.

"Seriously, dude. That's not a good idea," Briggs added.

"But they'll take care of this. It's what they do."

"And then what?" Knight walked over to Caleb, placing his hand on his friend's shoulder. "Then we will all be in their debt. If it was a choice between my uncle and your parents, no offense, but I'd pick the mayor."

Caleb nodded. "I get it, but what the fuck can we do?" He pointed to the ceiling. "What's going to happen when Seraphina or Mr. Hillingham notice Mrs. Hillingham is missing?"

"I got the impression Mr. Hillingham isn't really around much," I said, remembering all the talks with Seraphina and her utter resentment of her father.

"But what about Seraphina? Or that stupid luncheon that's going on right now?" Caleb took something out of his back pocket and shoved it in Knight's hand. "Here's your evidence of what went down. But who do we give it to?"

"I'll figure that out later. Right now, we have to get out of here. I don't think it's a good idea to lock her in here, Violet. I know you're angry, but that doesn't mean we should do to her what she was going to do to us," Knight said with soft eyes.

I ground my teeth. He was right, and I hated him for it. I wanted to beat that woman and leave her for dead. She didn't care about me, and she used my pain to manipulate me. Trying to be a mother figure and offer me advice, all while she was planning to kill me.

And I fell for it so easily.

I stared down at her messy brown hair as it covered her face and frowned. Was I angry at her for wanting to murder me, or was I irritated at myself for believing her lies?

"Fine." I folded my arms over my chest. "But can I at least spit on her?"

I heard some chuckles, and the corner of Knight's lips curled. "Sure. Hock a loogie on that bitch."

And that was exactly what I did. After inhaling all the dust from the boxes in the room, it was big and disgusting. Perfect for her.

We left her there. We would not lock her in the room, but that didn't mean we would do anything to help her, either.

The only way out of the basement was the way I came in. We made a plan to slip out individually. That way, if someone came near, it would be easier to hide.

Caleb was first. If someone saw him, they might not think much of it. Of all the families, his was the wealthiest. From what Knight told me, Caleb's family was old money—old crime money.

We waited about five minutes, and then Briggs left.

"You nervous?" Knight asked as we stood on one of the top steps near the basement door.

"A little . . . but I'm also relieved to be out of that room. I really thought I would die there." A sudden wave of emotion came over me.

I tried to swallow back the tears, but it wasn't happening. Exhaustion mixed with fear was causing my body to break.

Knight took a step forward and pulled me into an embrace. "I'd never let that happen. I told you I'd protect you."

A sob escaped, and my body shook. I was tired of fighting. All I wanted out of life was to be an average teenager. To go to school and complain about homework and go to the movies with my friends. Simple shit. Yet here I was, trying to escape death. Running from being locked away by a psycho because of something I had nothing to do with.

I pulled back after a minute and wiped away my tears. "Maybe I should leave. Move someplace where they can't find me."

"Where's that?" Knight leaned down, wiping away a tear with his thumb. "They have money. They have resources. And they have access to the police. I don't know of a place you could go where they won't track you down. Believe me, I wish I did. I'd go with you, take Ava, and we could all live a peaceful life together."

Damn, that sucked.

"Then what should I do?"

"For right now, just keep going about your business. Go to school and hang out with Arabella. Do normal shit. Don't let on that you may know anything."

"But Seraphina told me so much. She knows I'm not naïve. And once her mom wakes up, she'll come after me. She wants me dead."

Knight's brows creased. "But why?"

I sighed and reached under my dress to pull the photograph I found in the box from my bra. "This is why."

I lifted it to Knight. His mouth fell open, and he took it from my fingers. "That's Jack Franklin. Wow . . . he's so young here. He looks around our age."

"Yeah." I pointed to the woman in the picture. "And that's my mom."

His eyes slowly lifted to me. "So, you're—"

"Jack Franklin's daughter. In the flesh." I waved my hands in the air.

His head fell back. "Oh my god. This makes so much sense now."

"Can you fill me in? Because I'm still lost."

His lips thinned, and he gave me back the photo. "I don't really have time to explain it right now. But I promise, I'll show you everything once we get home. You're the missing link, Violet. You're the key to the lockbox that is this crazy, fucked-up adventure."

"You call it adventure; I call it hell."

"That fits better. You're the key to hell." He smirked.

I narrowed my eyes. "You're the worst."

"It's been about five minutes. It's time to go. I'll wait here just in case someone sees you," Knight said as he patted my shoulder.

Sucking in a fortifying breath, I reached for the door handle. Slowly, I pushed open the door. Pressing my ear to the opening, I heard nothing.

Glancing back, I saw Knight urge me on with a wave of his hand. *Right. You got this, Violet.*

Quickly as I could manage, I slipped out the door, closing it behind me. No one was around.

I crept along the wall, nearly knocking a painting off in the process. Wincing, I grabbed the frame and stopped the swaying artwork.

Once I got to the edge of the wall, I

looked around. No one was there. But as I moved closer to the door, I saw movement on the outside. There were two large windows on either side of the door.

Guests were arriving. When I heard the doorbell, I gasped.

Shit.

I darted back behind the stairs by the basement door. After a few moments, I heard the door open and then people talking.

How was I supposed to get out of here?

That was when I remembered the garage. There was a door in the garage, but I had to walk through the kitchen to get there. I sank back, slowly stepping past the basement door and farther down the hall.

I heard the clinking of dishes, and the scent of garlic filled the air. Glancing over my shoulder, I saw servers and kitchen staff scurrying around a marble counter.

Just before I turned to slip into the kitchen, I saw a figure at the end of the hall. My heartbeat filled my ears. Thankfully, the person who just arrived hadn't seen me.

Ichabod King.

A squeak escaped my lips, and I jumped into the kitchen before he could see who made that sound. Some staff stared at me, but most of them ignored me. Glancing down, I realized I must have looked awful. There were stains on my dress and a cut on my leg.

My hand went to my chest. The pendant . . . it was gone.

"Shit," I muttered under my breath.

It must have slipped off in the basement. I couldn't go back for it *ever.*

Seraphina's shrill voice slapped me out of thoughts about Knight's mom's necklace. I had to get out of here.

I scurried down the hall and through the garage door. Within moments, I was in the driveway, mixing in with the guests who were still arriving.

As I walked back to Knight's house, I was thankful it was so close. I kept looking back, hoping to find Knight. And when I didn't, I thought maybe he drove past me when heading back and would wait for me at the house.

But Knight wasn't there when I arrived. The home was eerily silent.

All I wanted to do was collapse into my bed and sleep, but the worry that Knight was caught kept my eyes from shutting.

FOUR

Knight

I HEARD SOME MOVEMENT by the basement door a minute after Violet left, so I stayed a little longer in the stairwell.

I opened the door after a few minutes and saw that no one was around. Just as I was about to step out, I saw movement.

After closing the door, I ran back down the stairs.

The door to the basement opened, and I glanced around to find a place to hide. I had no choice; I ran back to the room Violet had been locked inside.

There was a voice. It was deep and made my blood curdle.

My uncle.

"I have to make appearances, Kiki. That's part of our deal. You are the arm candy that makes me look good. So, where the fuck are you?"

I sucked in my breath, trying not to make a sound.

"With her? Can't you stop eating pussy for one minute and play the part as my fucking wife? It's what I pay you for. Unless you want this deal to end ... which also means the Elicit deal, too. I can easily draw up new paperwork and make sure you are no longer a partner of our little venture."

Elicit? How was he involved with that illegal drug? I had glanced at the folder Edwin gave me and saw the drug name in there, but I hadn't read it yet.

Once I got out of here, I was going to read everything Edwin had given me.

"Tell Janice you need to do your fucking job for once. Get over to the Hillingham's. Now!" my uncle yelled.

There was silence for a moment, and then I heard him walk closer to me. I glanced around to look for a place to hide. The only things that would block me were boxes. With how they were scattered around the room, it would take too long and cause too much noise.

I was screwed.

My uncle would discover me, and there was nothing I could do about it.

"What the hell—" I heard him mumble as he stood in the doorway and glanced up at me.

The look of surprise on his face was different, something I wasn't used to. The man always appeared as if he knew what he was doing. And as much as I hated him, I learned something very useful from my uncle—always look like you know what you're doing, even if you don't.

"Knight." He slipped his hands into the pockets of his navy slacks.

Ichabod King was wearing his mayoral suit today. Navy, perfectly tailored, with a crisp, white button-up and red tie. The typical American politician suit. The red, white, and blue going over well with his constituents.

I hated it. It reminded me of what a self-serving liar he was, and how he only cared about what could make him money.

"Uncle," I responded.

His gray eyes flickered to Crystal's body, and I knew it was my turn to be surprised. The corner of his lips curled. Was he happy she had been knocked out?

He pointed down at her. "You did this?"

"No, I didn't. Don't worry, she's only knocked out. I checked her pulse."

Because I would never want to murder anyone, unlike the other people in the room.

He sighed. "Too bad. Just makes my job tougher."

What the hell . . .?

I narrowed my eyes. "Are you planning to kill Mrs. Hillingham?"

He pinched the bridge of his nose. Was I annoying him by asking him questions? I guessed murder was no big deal for him, kind of like ordering a latte at The Drip.

"Son, you have—"

"I'm not your son," I gritted my teeth and took a step forward as my jaw tensed. "I had a father. Remember? Your brother. The one you murdered."

"I didn't murder your father. He went down in a plane. Do you need to go back to Green Meadows for a while?" His brows rose in mock concern.

"Fuck that place and fuck you." I took another step, my foot just an inch from Crystal's head. "You're just pissed I didn't fall for your adoption plan. It's interesting how the adoption agency wanted you to show interest in me. That outburst at the agency worker was all you."

His nose flared. "You told her to ask me about the town center plan, knowing it was falling apart. You knew it would upset me."

Yeah, I did.

In his first year as mayor, he had the grandiose plan of revitalizing the town center with new shops and a walkable trail around Happy Pond. But red tape and some local people who had money didn't want it to happen. It eventually fell to pieces, and he looked like a failure— something my uncle hated.

He always desperately needed to appear smart, a winner, and in control.

I shrugged. "But you're so smart, Uncle. You should have known I'd screw it all up."

"You fucking little shit." He lunged forward, almost stepping on Crystal, and tried to grab my shirt.

I shuffled back in time and laughed.

"You're a total fuckup, you know that? You wanted my parents' house, but I got it. You wanted Ava, but I'm her legal guardian. You wanted Violet, but she lives with *me*."

He turned his gaze from me and shook

his head. "I wanted none of those things. What I wanted was to get rid of them." He turned back to face me, his eyes filled with hate. "They were a problem that needed a solution. But now they're your problem."

What was he going on about?

"You wanted to kill Ava?"

He tilted his head from side to side. "Eventually. A natural progression. She gets sick, ends up in the hospital, and then dies because she's just too weak."

I clenched my fists and moved toward him. That fucker needed to go down. I aimed my fist for his face, but he was expecting it. He dodged to the side, causing me to miss.

"I don't know why you're so upset. I didn't do it. I only wanted her because I could get her inheritance. But now, I don't need that, or your money, for that matter. Maybe even Violet's money."

My head went back in surprise. "Violet's money? She doesn't have any money. She doesn't even own a car."

"Oh for fuck's sake, Knight. Haven't you figured it out by now? She's Jack Franklin's daughter."

I sighed. "But that doesn't mean she's rich. If Jack wanted her in his life, or even to help Violet and her mom, they wouldn't have been living in a trailer park."

There was silence as he stared at me. The way he looked at me was like a scientist studying a lab rat.

"Sure, let's go with that," he said and waved me out of the room. "If you don't mind, I need to take care of Crystal."

"You can't kill her."

"And why can't I? She's a murderer, Knight. She killed the driver of the bus that went off the side of the mountain with Violet inside. She's not a good person."

"She's a mother. And a human being."
I waved my hands in the air, confused why
he saw nothing wrong with it.

"Yes . . . Seraphina. She's as bad as her
mom. Look, how about I promise that I
won't kill her if you don't tell anyone you
saw me down here. Okay?"

"Okay," I lied.

"And don't worry . . . I'm not coming
after you," he said with a sigh.

"I know you won't."

He narrowed his eyes at me, suddenly
suspicious that I agreed with him so easily.

"How do you know?"

"Because, Uncle, I got information on
you. Things that, upon my death, my
lawyers are instructed to release to various
sources. The media, the internet. And no
amount of cleanup will stop the public
from wanting to burn you at the stake."

His eyes darted around the room. My

uncle, the guy who had control of every situation he was a part of, was worried I now had the upper hand.

And to be honest, he should have been scared, because what I had on him would ruin his life for years. But I wasn't a fool. I would keep that information to myself until it was the right time to let it out.

There were some things I needed to know before he went down. Like if he was the one responsible for the plane crash that killed Jack Franklin and my parents.

"Anything you have on me, I'll deny. It's the word of a teenager, spoiled with money, who had to spend time in a psych ward, against the pillar of the community. And I'm pretty sure I know who the public will believe." He smirked as if he had me beat.

Let him believe that. I was patient.

My eyes drifted to Crystal, and I

noticed something glitter near her foot. The necklace I gave Violet before she left for the luncheon.

As I lifted my gaze to my uncle, his face filled with concern, no matter how much he masked it with a sleazy smile. I knew it was time to leave.

"About Crystal—"

"She's not your concern." His eyes swept her body.

I frowned. The way he watched her was the same way he looked at Violet the day I caught him and his buddies in the pool house.

Revolting.

I took a step closer to him. "Look, you need to leave."

Crystal was a bitch who deserved to be in jail, but I wasn't about to leave her here with my rapey uncle.

"Fine." He smiled with a sudden

change in demeanor. "Let's head up to the party together."

I narrowed my eyes and wondered why he gave up so easily.

"I'm sure Crystal will wake up with an intense headache, and by that time, the party will be in full swing. And you'll be long gone."

It was almost like he was helping me. But why?

"Okay."

We left the room and headed up the stairs, mixing in with the guests once we entered the foyer. I didn't leave, not right away. I decided it would be best if I stayed near my uncle.

I deduced that he wanted me out of the basement so he could have his way with Crystal—and God only knew what else.

But Ichabod King surprised me. Kiki showed up, and they were linked arm and arm for about a half hour. Then, as the clock struck four in the afternoon, they left the party.

With them gone, I was set to leave as well. Mrs. Hillingham never made an appearance, and I worried that bump on her head was worse than I had originally thought.

I slipped down to the basement before leaving and was surprised to find she wasn't there. The door to the room was locked. I banged on it in case she had moved and knocked the door closed by accident.

But there was no response. Maybe she woke up and slipped up to her bedroom, and I just hadn't noticed. That was a possibility since the luncheon was crowded.

Crystal was obviously conscious enough to leave the basement, and my uncle had left, so there was no reason to stay.

I shrugged and left. It was time to head home and check on Violet.

FIVE

Violet

MY WET HAIR FELL down my back as I pulled the towel from my head. It felt good to wash off the grime of Seraphina's basement.

Leaning over the sink, I wiped the fog from the mirror. There, staring back, was a girl completely lost. The more I stumbled upon the truths about my life, the farther into the wilderness I sank.

I had a father. Jack Franklin.

"Violet Franklin," I mumbled to myself.

That could have been my name. My brow creased. Something kept my parents apart.

And that was when the most obvious and depressing thought came to me.

Drugs.

"Of course. No wonder his family wanted nothing to do with her. My mom was an addict, not to be trusted."

I scrunched up my face. I loved that woman, but she had fucked up so much. Her actions had ruined so many lives. I didn't want to hate her, but at that moment, I couldn't help but start to.

My head swiveled toward the

bathroom door. There was a noise coming from my bedroom. It sounded like something fell.

When I opened the door, cool air wafted in, causing my skin to prickle. Someone was lying on my bed.

"Hello?"

Knight stared at the towel wrapped around my body as he sat up. "Hello."

"What are you doing in my room?"

My heart was beating wildly, but I refused to let him know what he was doing to me. I leaned against the bathroom door and folded my arms. I tried not to stare at his lips as they curled.

He got up and meandered toward me, looking every bit the devil. His hair was wild, and his eyes darkened, focusing on my tits while his fingers yanked at his collar.

At first, I thought he was tugging at his

top in irritation, but when he pulled it off, I realized it wasn't the shirt that was bothering him. He reached for me, and with one flick of his finger, my towel fell.

"What the fuck?" I gazed at the heap on the floor in surprise.

"Exactly." He grabbed the back of my neck and pulled me to him.

Knight's lips crashed into mine. I fought. My hands pressed against his chest, but it was all an act . . . and he knew it.

My entire body came alive when his hand cupped my tit, his thumb grazing my nipple.

His mouth became greedy, nipping at my lips. I gasped, and he took advantage, his tongue plunging inside.

I shouldn't want him. Crave him. There were still so many questions unanswered. And what Seraphina said to me back in her basement rang true.

Why was Knight at Happy Pond the night my mom died?

But the more his fingers curled into my flesh, the less I thought about those questions. My hand went to his head, and I slipped my fingers through his silky waves. A boy shouldn't have hair this soft; it should be against the law. But even if it were a crime, I was sure Knight would happily commit it and never worry about getting arrested.

His lips pulled free, and Knight stared down at me with heat in his eyes. "God damnit, Violet. From now on, you don't go anywhere without my okay. You got that?"

He just dumped a glass of ice water on me with that statement.

I pushed back. "You must be joking?"

"I'm so fucking serious. You could have been killed. If I hadn't placed that

recording device in my mom's necklace—
"

"So you admit it." I pushed my finger into his chiseled chest. "You were listening to me. Spying on me like a creeper."

His brows shot up. "More like someone who was protecting you. And if I hadn't done that, you'd still be in that basement."

I snorted and rolled my eyes. Everything he said was true, but the fact that he did it without my knowledge was insane.

"You could have told me."

He rubbed the back of his neck. "And then what? You would have agreed to go along with recording your time at the party?"

No. I would have thought he was crazy for even thinking it.

"Maybe." I shrugged. "You don't know until you ask."

His eyes slid down my body like a snake, and I felt every slither.

"I've protected you at every turn. I found you in the boys' locker room just a few weeks after you started at Green Hills, and did I destroy you?"

My face heated. I couldn't look at him. Staring at the floor, I replied, "No." It was barely a whisper.

He moved forward, and I backed up until my ass hit the bathroom counter. His hips pushed into me. The hardness covered by his jeans ground into me. Knight was reminding me who he was and what I did to him.

"And what did I do to you, Violet?" His voice lowered to a rumbling whisper that was both a threat and a tease.

"You, uh . . ." I swallowed, barely able to respond, "you licked me."

His hand went up to my chin. I winced

as he dug his finger into my skin, forcing me to tilt my head up.

"I devoured you." He moved closer to my ear. "And you loved it."

I whimpered. My nipples were already hard spikes as they rubbed against his chest. I shifted from the pain of being pinned against the counter, but also to ease the ache between my legs.

His hands grabbed my hips, pushing me farther up onto the counter. Knight lifted my legs until my feet were set firmly on the counter, and I was spread wide for him.

And I hated that I let him. Hated that I wanted it. To show him what he did to my body.

His eyes dipped down as he took a step back. My clit twitched as his finger slid around my thigh and down over my wet folds.

I hissed at the raw sensation.

"You get so wet, Violet. God, I fucking love it." Knight reached into his pocket and retrieved a condom. I stared in wonderment as he unbuttoned his jeans and released his cock. Though I had seen it so many times, it still made me shiver.

He rolled on the condom, but instead of moving forward to push inside me, Knight got down on his knees.

"You want it again? You want me to devour you?" His hands gripped my thighs as his thumbs rubbed around my clit. I could barely concentrate on his words as he toyed with me.

I bit my lip and nodded—it was the best I could do. His hot breath and whatever he was doing with his thumbs stole my voice and my thoughts.

"That's what I expected." He lowered his face to my core and gave me the gentlest kiss. "You pretend that I don't affect you. But your beautiful, weeping pussy betrays you every time."

He was right. I tried not to like him, but as each day passed, I realized it was more than lust that brought us together. It was something I was too afraid to even imagine. Knight and I shared so much. Our past was connected in ways I never imagined.

And I wondered . . .. If things had been different . . .. If my father had a hand in raising me, would I have known him? Maybe I would have been his girlfriend last year, not Seraphina.

He flattened his tongue and made a show of licking me like an ice cream cone. My head fell back, hitting the mirror. It was working. It didn't matter how much he toyed with me or made me watch him as he devoured me, my body craved it.

I reached forward, tightening my fingers in his hair. He groaned. The sick fuck liked when I gave in to him. When my hips moved and my fingers curled, that was when he felt pleasure. That was his reward.

I arched my back when his fingers slipped inside me. My hips moved back and forth beyond my control. I felt myself tighten around his fingers. It wouldn't be long.

"Fuck," I spit out as if the word alone would make me come.

"Soon," Knight said between pants.

I took a deep breath, and the room smelled of soap and my sex. When I released the breath, it came as a groan. My movements were erratic, and despite the humidity in the bathroom, my skin pebbled.

"Fuck, I'm coming."

My climax slammed into me, and all I heard was Knight's groans as he lapped me up. My core was still twitching when he stood. My body was in the throes of orgasm, and I sat there helpless as he lined his cock up to my opening.

He didn't ask, and I wasn't about to tell him no if he had. Knight slammed into me—no subtlety or romance.

But that wasn't the boy's style. He was the devil, and I had to take what he threw at me.

His fingers grabbed my wrists and held them down as he pumped into me. He watched me with hooded eyes, sometimes my face and other times my tits as they bounced from his force.

And the whole time my pussy wanted more. I wanted to reach between my legs and flick my clit. I wanted to come again all over his cock. I wanted to let him know how much I enjoyed the way he used my body.

But I couldn't do that.

"Say it," he sneered.

His voice was an erotic toy that made my core tighten once more.

I knew exactly what he wanted me to say. My usual instinct to quarrel with him was a rubbery mess on the floor. I had no fight left in me. He worked it out of me with his fingers, his mouth, and his enormous cock.

"Do what you want to me. You feel incredible," I said between pants.

His nose flared, and in a matter of seconds, he stopped and slipped his cock out of me. Letting go of my wrists, he pushed my legs wider. His thumb slid over my wet pussy and down to my asshole.

I bit my lip, watching him.

"Please," I begged like the greedy girl

he wanted.

His gaze flickered up to me. "Is that what you want? For me to fuck you right there?"

He fisted his cock, lining it to my puckered hole, and my heart thumped loudly in my chest.

It was one thing to have his thumb there, but his cock . . .? That thing was huge.

"I don't know . . .."

He smirked and reached over, sliding open a drawer and pulling out a tube of something. Knight opened it and squeezed a clear, thick liquid into his hand, which he rubbed over my puckered hole.

It was warm, which surprised me. And something about that caused my apprehension to melt away. I reached down and slipped two fingers inside my pussy, fucking myself.

"I'll take that as a yes."

I nodded as my thumb swiped my clit, watching him align his cock with my asshole. He pushed, and my eyes widened. It hurt, an intense burning.

I shook my head, about to tell him to stop, but he kept pushing forward, and the burning died away. What replaced it was a feeling of fullness that caused my eyes to roll back into my head.

I tried to speak, but all that came out was a moan.

"Fuck, you're so tight," Knight said as his jaw clenched.

After a few seconds, he moved in and out of me. I already felt my core tightening. I was going to come again.

I worked my fingers in rhythm with his cock.

"Knight," I said with a groan.

My orgasm came suddenly. It was

intense. I cried out, my hips flexing as I rode it.

"Shit. I don't even need the lubricant with how much you're creaming yourself."

I felt it too, all over my hand—which Knight grabbed and shoved my fingers inside his mouth to suck.

My climax lingered longer than any other. But as high as my body floated from the euphoria of the moment, I saw when Knight came.

He watched me with hooded eyes as his orgasm slammed into his body. His face contorted into bliss. His hips slowed, and he rode out the wave. And when it was nearly complete, he leaned over and kissed me savagely. His lips sought mine as if I would save him.

The kiss turned from ravenous to sweet within moments. Knight wrapped his arms around me. When he broke the kiss, he moved down my chin to my neck.

I smiled, and my heart fluttered. The moment was too beautiful to last, that I knew. But I was going to enjoy every second for as long as it was only us.

He broke our embrace to slide out of me and clean up. Knight even dampened a cloth to wipe me. Then he picked me up in his arms like some noble prince and brought me to my bed.

After placing me there, he curled up beside me. "You fit perfectly in my arms . . . like you were meant to be there all along," he whispered in my ear.

"This feels good. Why don't we do this more often?"

His finger slid up and down my arm, causing gooseflesh to break out. "Because it usually ends in a fight. You don't trust me, so at some point, you say something that makes it obvious that you don't want me around."

Another frosty glass of water to ruin the moment.

I shifted around to face him. "So it's my fault? If you would just be honest with me, tell me why you spy on me without my knowledge. . . then none of that would happen."

"Then it wouldn't be spying, would it?" he said without a hint of humor in his voice.

I frowned and opened my mouth to respond, but he beat me to it. "You're right, Violet. It took me having you in my life for the past two months for me to realize that you're as affected by all this as I am. What is it you want to know?"

My mouth fell open as my mind went blank. I hadn't expected him to agree; I thought we'd fight like always. I glanced around, hoping to come up with a question when one thing kept popping up. "Why were you at Happy Pond when my mom died?"

He sighed. "I'll tell you . . . but you won't like it."

SIX

Violet

KNIGHT'S WORDS REPEATEDLY RANG in my ears. He was right; I didn't like what he told me about the night my mom died.

"What's wrong?" Arabella asked as we walked up to the school entrance the Monday after my almost-tragic weekend.

"Why do you ask?" I kept my gaze averted, choosing to stare at the gleaming, expensive cars in the parking lot.

"You haven't answered a single question about the luncheon on Saturday or said more than hi since you got in my car this morning. Is this because I bailed on you on Sunday? I told you that—"

"No, I'm sorry. It's not because you bailed." I sighed, realizing it was hypocritical of me to expect honesty from Knight but then not be true to my best friend. "Some things happened this weekend . . . crazy shit. And I'm a little confused right now as to where I stand in this world." I groaned and shook my head. "That made little sense, didn't it?"

She stopped me and pulled me aside. We were in the grass by the bushes that lined the wall of the front of the building. "Did Seraphina do something to you? I knew she was fake-friending you." Then she gasped, her eyes widening. "Or did the mayor show up? I think he's friends with the Hillinghams, so that's totally possible."

I placed my hands on her shoulder. "Yes and no."

I knew I had no choice but to explain what happened at the party.

"Holy shit!" Her eyes traveled my body. "And you're not hurt?"

"No."

"And Jack Franklin was your father. That's crazy. But it makes sense why the mayor wanted you to live with him."

I tilted my head. "Why?"

"The money, of course. That man was stupid rich. He fell in the class of untouchable. Even other wealthy people had to do whatever he said. Shit, even politicians knew not to cross him."

"Then why did my mom struggle?

Why did he not once try to contact me?"

My mom went on and on about how he loved her and me, but other people kept them apart. Like they were Shakespearian and shit.

Arabella frowned and tugged on her red braid. "I don't know. I wish I did. At least you know who your father is now. That has to make you feel a little better."

I nodded, but it was a lie. If anything, it brought up more questions.

"I asked Knight why he was at Happy Pond the night my mom died . . . and he finally told me."

Her hand made a circle. "And . . .? You don't just drop a bomb like that and then stop talking, Violet."

I chuckled. "Okay. He was there because of his friend Edwin. Edwin was there to meet someone, but he didn't know who. Knight thought it was my mom when she showed up. But Knight fucked it up and stepped on something that made a noise, so he had to lay low for a few minutes. By the time he stood back up, Edwin was hovering over a canoe."

"But isn't that where he found you?"

I nodded. "Yeah."

"So, Edwin killed your mom and put you in the canoe? Maybe it's a good thing he got arrested."

"That's what I thought too. But he made a noise again, and the guy ran off. Once he came out of the woods, that's when he found me. Edwin showed up a few minutes later, after Knight called the police. He confronted Edwin, but he swore he had just showed up. He wasn't the guy Knight was watching from the woods. It was someone else."

Arabella's lips thinned. "That sounds suspect."

"Right?" I nodded. "But Knight said Edwin was in completely different clothes than the guy he was watching from the woods. That guy was in all black with a hoodie, and Edwin wore a camel-colored wool coat."

Arabella stood silent for a minute.

"I think I'm as confused as before. Maybe even more so. Knight told me I would not like what he said, and he was right."

"I'm confused too. If Knight's right, then someone obviously killed your mom and was about to kill you. We just don't know who. If Knight's wrong, he's either covering for his friend, or it was . . ." she trailed off, not wanting to admit the last part.

"Or it was Knight who did it." I let out a bitter laugh. "Don't think I haven't had that same thought in my head for the last day and a half."

She chewed on her thumbnail, and I glanced around. Students were moving into school, ignoring us, except for one.

Seraphina's icy blue gaze settled on me.

"Shit," I said, and Arabella looked up.

"Oh, no." Arabella grabbed my arm. "She can't do anything. Not here where everyone will see. I think you're safe."

"Yeah, for now."

And then what? Would she point a gun at me like her mom? That bitch was crazy, and you know what they say . . . like mother, like daughter.

Seraphina stomped up to me, her eyes wild. "Where is she?"

"Who?"

"You fucking know who. My mom, you fucking idiot. She never showed up to the luncheon. Her own luncheon. I had to make excuses for her. Do you know how much I hated lying to those people?"

I rolled my eyes. I thought lying was her middle name.

"How the fuck should I know where she is? Last I checked, she wanted to kill me. As did you." I shoved my finger into her chest. It surprised me when one of her balloon tits didn't pop.

She smacked my hand away. Seraphina's eyes darted from me to Arabella.

"I have no idea what you're talking about. Just because you locked yourself in our basement after you went snooping around, that's not our fault."

"Wow, do you actually believe the lies coming out of your mouth? You hate lying to your mom's rich friends, but to me, it's okay. You're so phony."

"Why would I care what a poor little

piece of trash thinks?"

I guess her mom never told her I was Jack Franklin's daughter, or she wouldn't be calling me poor. Not that I had access to his money, but I suspected the mayor and even Crystal thought I did.

"You know she's Jack—" I placed a hand over Arabella's mouth before she let it out.

Seraphina folded her arms. "You two are weird."

"At least we're not murderers." I moved my hand away from Arabella and took a step toward Seraphina.

Her face flushed, and she fisted her hands by her side. "I'm not a murderer!"

Several kids turned to watch us.

"Are you sure your mom didn't run off, knowing she was in deep shit?" I asked with a smirk.

"Yeah, leaving whatever comes to light

on your shoulders. Like that bus driver who went missing. You know, the one who was conveniently out of sight when you locked Violet in the bus."

Seraphina's eyes widened. She knew something.

"Of course you both would be friends. Two horrible bitches like yourselves deserve each other," she said with a sneer before whirling around, her blond hair fanning the air before she marched off.

"That's crazy. I can't believe her mom disappeared. I thought you said Caleb had knocked her out when you left?"

"I did." I glanced around, looking for Knight. "When I left, she was still on the floor. I would think that if she woke up, she'd be too lightheaded to drive away. Someone must have seen her."

"Maybe Knight knows what happened to her." The way Arabella looked at me made me realize she was thinking the same thing as I was.

Knight had something to do with Crystal's disappearance.

I wrapped my arms around myself as a chill fell over me.

"Every single person who disappeared has either hurt me or was involved in hurting me. First, it was John Lenker. Then the bus driver. Now Seraphina's mom."

"What are you trying to say, Violet?" Arabella asked with a frown.

I didn't want to believe it, but the more I thought about the lies, the half-truths, and how Knight continuously held things back from me, the more it made sense.

"Even my mom," I said under my breath.

"What?"

"What if Knight was lying to me when

he told me someone else was there the night my mom died? What if Edwin wasn't there and didn't even show up later?"

"Why would he hurt your mom?"

"Maybe he knew I was Jack Franklin's daughter this entire time. Maybe he hated his uncle so much, he would do anything to hurt him. Even keep me at his side."

"But it's not like you control Franklin First. Or even have access to his money." Arabella rubbed her brow. "Wait . . . do you? Maybe there's a will."

I swallowed as the pieces to the puzzle of my life formed a picture, a picture that gave me everything I ever dreamed of growing up—money, power, and never having to worry where my next meal would come from. But it also turned me into a shiny golden object that everyone wanted to carry around in their pocket.

I hated doubting Knight, but the more

I learned, the less I trusted him. Yet I felt he was the only one who could protect me.

"I'm so fucked," I mumbled and felt a warm arm circle my shoulder.

Glancing up, Arabella gave me a soft, comforting smile. At least I had her. My only friend.

SEVEN

Violet

"I'M FINALLY HOME. ANYTHING happen while I was gone?" Aunt Dahlia asked as she pulled her black roller suitcase into the foyer of Knight's house.

"Wait." She held up her hands. "We still live here, right?"

I chuckled and ran over, throwing my arms around her waist. Her coat still held the chill from the early November air.

A week had passed since the luncheon, and Crystal was nowhere to be found. Seraphina threatened me all week at school, and then took advantage of every moment to make my life a living hell. It was like the first week of school all over again.

"Yes, we still live with Knight and Ava."

My aunt glanced around. "Where are they? I brought back some things to thank them for their hospitality." She bent down and unzipped the outer pockets of her luggage.

"Ava's in the kitchen having ice cream, as usual."

That girl lived off it. I swear, if they made an IV of ice cream, she'd beg her brother to get it for her.

As for Knight, he wasn't here this morning. I'd been avoiding him most of the week. He must have noticed since I woke this morning to a note. He told me to meet him at the diner, Jack's Place, later today.

"Wonderful. I'll go give her this." My aunt held up a doll that looked exactly like the evil White Witch from *The Lion, The Witch, and The Wardrobe*.

An unshed tear pricked my eye as I remembered my mom reading me that story when I was little—that happy, brief memory forgotten until now. I used to love how she read me stories before bed. For the past several years, I became too focused on the bad things she did that I forgot all the good.

"I think she'll—" My voice cracked, and I cleared my throat. "She'll love that."

"I know how much Ava loves evil queens, so I figured she might like this. And I also have your mom's old copy of the book."

My brows shot up. "Really? I'd love to

see it. Maybe I could read it to Ava . . . if she doesn't already know the story."

The thought warmed my heart. In a strange way, I would feel more connected to my mom if I passed on that story. Just the idea made me smile.

"That's a great idea. I bet Ava would love that. Let's go show her my gift and see if she's heard of the story."

My aunt stepped forward, placing her arm around my back. She gave me a comforting squeeze before we headed into the kitchen.

There, seated at the counter, was Ava, licking her fingertips. Half of her face was covered in chocolate, even the tip of her nose, which was impressive.

She looked up and smiled. "That was good. Now remember, Violet, you can't tell Knight, for I hold the bracelet in my hand."

I sighed. She snuck into my room while I was in the shower this morning. I'd been her slave all morning. Hence the ice cream.

"If you give me back my princess bracelet, I can let you have this evil White Witch doll." I waved my hand at the gift my aunt was holding up.

Ava's eyes rounded. She hopped off the barstool and threw my bracelet to me. I caught it in time and cringed at its stickiness.

She threw her arms up, expecting the present to fall into her hands like magic.

"Um, this is for little girls who have *clean hands*. And face." My aunt raised her brow.

Where my mom was a lot more carefree with how I was raised, my aunt believed in rules. For a young girl left alone to fend for herself, I loved that my aunt was strict.

I got the impression with the way Ava frowned and stomped her feet that she wasn't a fan of discipline.

"But I gave back the bracelet. That's enough. I don't want to wash my hands and face."

"Seems like someone's had too much sugar." My aunt slid her eyes to me.

I shrugged. I was only eighteen. What did she want?

Ava's lower lip wobbled. Was she about to cry? My heart raced in fear. I never meant to upset her.

"Crying won't help your cause." My aunt stood firm.

And like magic, Ava's lips thinned. With a loud groan, the little girl stalked to the corner of the kitchen and grabbed the step stool, bringing it to the kitchen sink.

A minute later, Ava stood in front of my aunt with clean hands, face, and a look that said if she didn't get the doll, there would be hell to pay.

"One doll for one sweet little girl." My aunt smiled down at Ava, placing the White Witch in her hands.

But before Ava could run off with it, my aunt added, "And what do you say when someone gives you something?"

Ava tilted her head in confusion.

"You say thank you," Dahlia mentioned after a few moments when Ava would not respond.

"Thank you," Ava said with a smile. She then took the doll and ran out of the room.

"I don't think that girl has learned any manners." My aunt stared at the doorway Ava just ran through moments ago.

"Well, her parents died two years ago when she was only four, and from what I gather, the mayor and his wife helped little in raising her. It was all left up to Knight, who was only sixteen at the time."

A pained expression settled on my aunt's face. "So much death. It's hard enough when you're an adult dealing with the death of a loved one, but when you're a child . . ." Dahlia shook her head and placed her arm around me.

I held my breath and wondered if I should tell her. She had been traveling most of the past two months and didn't know all that had happened. She knew some, but not the full extent of evil that had been my life here in North Green Hills.

"I just want to apologize again for leaving you with the mayor. If I had known he was so neglectful, I never would have—"

"Stop. You had no idea. Neither did I when I came here."

"At least you got invited to apply to Winter River University. Speaking of which, when do you actually apply?"

Despite the chaos of my life, I had been working hard to get the application in order and writing my essay.

"I am planning to apply next week," I said before I bit my lip. "Hopefully, I find out if I'm in or not next month, in

December."

She held up both hands, crossing her fingers. "If you need any help with it, just let me know."

As nervous as I was about getting into Winter River University, I was more worried about letting my aunt in on my life here in the past two months.

"Can I talk to you about Mom?"

Her brow crinkled, and she nodded. "Of course you can. Anytime."

She waved me over to the bar chairs by the kitchen island counter.

"Since I've moved up here, I've learned some things about her. About me. And about her death."

Dahlia reached for my hand, clasping it between both of hers. "Okay."

I trembled, but I held her gaze. "I know who my father is."

I thought talking about this with her would be easier, but I was more nervous than my first day at Green Hills Academy.

"Really? All I knew was that he was some rich guy who walked away when he found out she was pregnant with you. I know she loved him, but I found it strange she hid her relationship from me. From everyone. That's why I thought he might be married or just embarrassed that she wasn't wealthy like him."

I could tell my aunt felt regret for thinking ill of my dad, and I didn't blame her for judging him harshly. If that was all I knew about him, I'd hate him too.

"There's a reason Mom hid him from me and from you. My dad was Jack Franklin."

My aunt's emerald eyes widened. "You mean the one who was head of Franklin First?"

I nodded and stayed quiet, letting her digest the recent information.

"But he's dead," she said, more to herself than to me.

"I know. He died in the same plane

crash that took Knight and Ava's parents."

My aunt's eyes flickered from me to the doorway of the kitchen and back again. "Wait, so they both knew each other? And the mayor is their uncle?"

I kept nodding. She was getting it.

"That seems . . . that's a coincidence." She stared at me, her eyes darkening. "Do you think that's why the mayor wanted you to live here? To take care of you?"

"Yes, I do. I also don't think Mom committed suicide. I think she was murdered, just as Knight thinks the plane crash that killed his parents and my dad wasn't an accident."

She gasped. "You don't think the mayor had anything to do with it, do you?"

I shrugged. "I don't know. What I do know is that the bus accident wasn't an accident. And the mayor wasn't exactly nice to me while he lived here."

"Oh no. Here I thought I was helping you by sending you up north, but all I did was put you in danger."

"I'm not blaming you. I just want you to know the truth."

She sighed and reached for the sticky bracelet I had tossed onto the counter once Ava left.

"Then you should also know something . . .. Your mom told me and made me promise not to say anything. And I hadn't really thought about it until now."

"What?"

"Your mom didn't get you this bracelet. A man came to the trailer over two years ago with a package. She told me, according to the note, that it was to be given to you for your eighteenth birthday."

"But Mom gave it to me on my sixteenth birthday . . .."

She got up and took the bracelet to the sink and rinsed it off. "I know. It was from your father." My aunt watched me as she rubbed the soapy jewelry in her hand.

"I thought Mom picked it up in the discount section of a store. But if it's from my father, then that means . . ." My words faded on my lips.

I blinked at the shiny jewels that Dahlia was wiping down with a tea towel.

"That they're real. Probably." She chuckled as she walked back to me, placing the bracelet in my hand. "That's why, when you threw it in the woods after your mom died, I picked it up. There was no way I was letting you leave behind something as precious as this. Of course, at the time, I didn't think it was real. I believed it was precious because it was from your father."

I turned the jewelry around in my hand. It must have been genuine gold with dangling emeralds, sapphires, and diamonds. I swallowed. "I can't believe I let Ava play with it."

"You didn't know."

"But why did it show up a year early?"

My aunt shrugged. "I think the company in charge of delivering it got the years mixed up. Probably because Jack had just died. Maybe there was a clause that stated they must deliver it upon his death."

I nodded. That must have been the reason. My finger slid over the smooth golden key on the bracelet. "Maybe it's the key to my dad's heart," I mumbled to myself.

The heart he could never let me see.

Dahlia's eyes narrowed, and she held out her hand. "Can I see that?"

I plopped the only valuable thing I owned into my aunt's hand.

"This is an actual key, Violet. It's not just a charm. See these notches? This unlocks something."

I took the bracelet back and studied the key. My heart pounded in my ears. My aunt was right.

This key opened something. But what?

E I G H T

Knight

I SAT IN THE corner of The Drip and lifted my eyes to the woman with shoulder-length red hair who told me she had all the answers.

Georgia Ellis.

"Thank you for meeting me this

morning. I was worried you wouldn't show," I said as I picked at the paper cozy that covered my coffee cup.

"There was no way I'd miss meeting with you, Mr. King."

I flinched. It felt strange hearing that title. A few people had addressed me as Mr. King over the past few months, but when I heard it, I always thought of my father.

"Please, call me Knight."

She nodded and then glanced around the shop. For a Saturday morning, The Drip was busy. So far, I had seen no one I knew, which was exactly what I wanted.

"So, tell me why you wanted to meet in such a public setting?" My eyes kept flicking to the door each time it opened.

I was nervous. The past two years of my life had been crazy, but rarely was I on edge. Angry, yes. Determined, absolutely. But never worried.

It was a feeling I avoided whenever

possible. So being on display for any of my uncle's minions to catch me with the journalist he loved to hate wasn't something I had desired on a Saturday morning.

"He can't do anything to us with so many witnesses around."

I knew who she meant. My uncle.

"No, he'll just wait until we're alone, and then one of us, or perhaps both of us, will disappear. Much like what happened to Crystal Hillingham."

She leaned across the table and lowered her voice. "So you know he had something to do with her disappearance."

I raised a brow and reached into my pocket. Sliding the thumb drive across the table, I said, "I think you're going to want to listen to this."

Since the necklace I gave Violet had a recording device on it, and I left it in the Hillingham's basement, it recorded everything that had happened. Once I listened to what my uncle did once I left, I knew I had to pass it on to Ms. Ellis.

"Why don't you go to the police?" She slid her fingers over mine, discreetly taking the drive from me and placing it in the pocket of her gray wool jacket.

"Who do you think gave me your information? The mayor just about owns all the cops in this town. But there was one who helped me."

She studied me for a moment. "Did you know the crash that killed your parents wasn't an accident?"

My heart beat a little faster. Finally, someone who understood.

"I had my suspicions. My uncle kept talking about a plan when he discussed the plane crash or me and my sister."

"He said that to you?"

I shook my head. "No. I overheard him a few times two years ago."

"So, you haven't heard anything since?"

I frowned. "He doesn't trust me anymore. Not when he thinks I'm trying to kill him."

Her eyes widened. "And are you?"

"No, of course not. I may be related to the man, but it doesn't mean I think like him."

"Then you should have this." She reached into her purse and pulled out an envelope.

"What's this?" I took it and shoved it inside my jacket pocket.

"It's all the information I've gathered over the last year about that plane crash. The mechanic who died? The day before the crash, his bank account was credited a hundred thousand dollars."

"Really?" That was new information.

"Not only that, but the toxicology report on his blood alcohol level from the car crash that killed him last year . . . the one that said he had a blood alcohol level of 0.13..."

"Yes, I got that report."

"It's wrong. It was faked. The real one is in that envelope." She jerked her chin in the direction of my coat pocket.

My head was swimming with all the extra information I was given. The never-ending marathon for the truth was starting to end, and I saw the finish line.

"Thank you so much. And just so you know, the memory stick I just gave you . . ." I pointed to the pocket she had tucked it inside. "I got some information off that bus driver's phone and found out my uncle turned the cancer drug Jack Franklin had worked on into that addictive drug Elicit."

Her eyes widened. "What we have on your uncle should put him away for a very long time. Let me work on putting the pieces together. In the meantime, see if you can find more evidence linking your uncle to these murders. The more evidence we have, the less he has to fight with."

I nodded as she stood.

"Let's get the bastard. I'm out of work because of him. No paper will touch me for fear of what Ichabod King would do to them."

"That's my plan."

"Just a warning . . . his wife isn't who she pretends to be."

She turned to leave but stopped. "One more thing. You might want to look into that new drug laboratory and manufacturing plant the mayor plans to open on the south side. Maybe that is linked to Elicit too." She winked and then headed toward the front door.

Taking a sip of my coffee, I scanned the room. Was anyone watching her or me? Was anyone leaving, following her out the door?

With everything she gave me, I should feel relief, but I was even more on guard. I was so close to bringing my uncle down that I knew anything could screw it up.

That meant I had to stay in my lane and not let my emotions mess anything up. It had hurt me when Violet avoided me this past week, but perhaps she was on to something.

I needed a strategy to make sure he couldn't get to me. I reached into my pocket to get out my phone when I heard a gasp. Glancing up, I noticed a few people point to their phones.

Something must have been trending on HitLoc, and based on their expressions, it wasn't good.

I opened the app and saw what had them so upset: a brief video of a leg sticking out of cement. The title of the video was "Another Man Found in Green Hills Academy Basement."

The hole that had been filled in—someone stuck a body in there before the cement could dry.

I quickly searched the internet for any

information on the body. When I discovered who it was, the blood drained from my face.

I placed my phone on the table and rubbed my face. As much as I didn't want to do it, I knew there was only one way I could stop my uncle.

Getting up, I grabbed my phone and coffee. As I made my way to the door, I tossed my drink in the trash and sent a quick text to my friends.

We needed to meet, and I worried it might be our last time together.

NINE

Violet

"ARE YOU SURE KNIGHT invited you too?" I asked as we walked up the steps into Jack's Place.

Arabella nodded. She was wearing dark skinny jeans that fit her perfectly with a leather bomber jacket, and her long red hair was tied back in a ponytail. She looked both cute and sexy at the same time, and I'd be lying if I said I wasn't a little jealous of her effortless style.

"I got a text about an hour ago from Knight. I assumed you got one too."

I shook my head. "No. He had already asked me this morning to meet him here. I didn't realize he knew about this place."

"Neither did I. Damn. Now that the secret is out, it won't be long before all of Green Hills Academy comes here."

I smiled. "I guess your little diamond in the rough will be no more."

She leaned over and grabbed the door handle, pulling it open. "Oh well. It was nice while it lasted."

We walked into the classic-looking diner. A warm feeling ran down my body. Comforting. That was what Jack's Place was, a place that felt like home.

I had only been here a few times since Arabella brought me two months ago.

Even if it was new to me, something about it felt like I had been coming here all my life.

"There he is." Arabella pointed to the corner.

I glanced over, and as Knight's steely gray eyes settled on me, a shiver ran straight to my core.

I both loved and hated how my body reacted to him. He had helped me so many times, but the thought that he might have had a hand in my mother's death lingered in the back of my mind.

I cared for Knight, my body longing for his, but could I trust him? That question never seemed to get answered.

"Thanks for coming. I invited the guys too. They should be here any minute." Knight waved at the booth seats.

I slid in, keeping my distance from Knight. But as much as I wanted space between us, I had to accept that my body would touch his when his friends showed up.

Both Caleb and Briggs were only moments behind us and slid into the booth, pushing me against Knight. Heat fanned my body as his thigh rubbed against mine. I kept my eyes straight ahead, never letting on that he was getting to me.

"Now that everyone is here, I wanted to let you in on what I've learned," Knight's deep voice rumbled, and I felt it in my core.

"Yeah, why are we meeting at this run-down place?" Caleb asked with a frown.

"Hey, I'll have you know that Jack's Place is amazing. You can apologize to me and this establishment once you've tried their biscuits and gravy sunny-side up." Arabella glared at Caleb.

"Whatever." He rolled his eyes, but I saw the corner of his mouth tick up for a second.

"Order us whatever you like, Arabella,

but I don't know how much of an appetite you are going to have once you hear there's been another body found in the Green Hills Academy basement."

I finally turned my head to face Knight. "What? But they filled the hole."

He nodded, his eyes dipping to my lips for a moment before he looked around the table. "Someone put the body in there while the cement was drying. Look."

Knight pulled out his phone, and we passed it around. When it got to me, I gasped. It was so ridiculous-looking that if someone didn't realize it was real, they'd have thought it was photoshopped.

Arabella narrowed her eyes at Knight. "I hadn't heard of this. How do you know, and I don't?"

I would have expected Arabella's dad, as the principal, to be the first to hear about it, and then, as nosy as his daughter was, she'd hear about it too.

"They found it this morning. I met

with a journalist right before I came here, and I noticed everyone at the coffee shop was murmuring about a dead body. The police are still at the school."

"I wonder who it is?" Briggs asked.

"It's the bus driver. Jewel's cousin."

I felt the blood drain from my face. "Oh, no."

Jewel was right to leave this place. How would she take it when she found out? My heart ached for her.

"Someone wanted to shut him up." Knight leaned in closer. "And I think that someone was my uncle."

A memory popped into my head. Something that had me questioning Knight.

"Arabella, when did they fill in the hole?"

She blinked and, after a moment, said, "Two weeks ago. It was that day we helped Jewel break into Green Hills."

The pieces were falling together. "And

didn't Jewel say she texted her cousin the next day and got no response?" I asked.

Arabella's head shot back. "You don't think she killed her own cousin?"

"No." I shook my head and glanced around the table. "You remember who we ran into after we helped Jewel get into the school? Crystal Hillingham."

Her eyes widened, and she whispered, "That's right."

"Oh, shit," Briggs commented.

"And she had on that rain slicker, remember?"

"Well, it had been raining earlier that evening," Arabella pointed out.

"I know, but it had those dark red splatters on it. She told me they were from the cupcakes, but now I wonder if it was blood."

"Then that means Crystal might have killed the bus driver and put his body in that hole," Knight said.

"The only problem is that Seraphina's

mom is missing too. So even if she killed the guy, there's no way they can arrest her. I bet she ran, knowing she was going to get caught eventually," Briggs added.

"Maybe. Until she's found, we can only guess if she did it or not," Arabella said with a sigh.

The server showed up at our table with multiple plates in her hand.

"We never ordered—" Caleb said but was quickly cut off.

"I did," Arabella said. "Knight told me to order whatever I wanted, so I got us each the best food on the menu."

"I didn't see you do that?" He narrowed his eyes at her, distrusting her ninja-like ordering skills.

"She knows me." Arabella winked at the waitress.

The server with gray bobbed hair winked back. She glanced around the table but cut back to me.

"What's your name?" she asked as she

tilted her head.

"Me?" I pointed to myself. "It's Violet."

Her sparkling blue eyes rounded. "Oh my god. I've seen you before when you came in here with Arabella, but I couldn't place you. Until now."

"Okay." I glanced around the table, everyone as confused as I was.

"Come with me." She waved for me to follow her.

Knight shifted out of the booth to let me out, and I scurried after the woman. I glanced back at the table. Arabella shrugged as if the waitress making me follow her was completely normal.

"I have something for you. The owner wanted you to have it."

My eyebrows shot up. "The owner. Who's the owner?"

We passed through some swinging green doors and made our way down a very narrow, short hallway.

"He was a very private person, so that's

not for me to say . . .." She took out a key chain from her apron pocket and unlocked a door.

"Wait right here, and I'll bring it to you."

She stepped inside the room and quickly shut the door behind her. I tried to take a peek but only saw a small desk before she closed the door.

After a minute she came back out again, closing the door before I saw anything in the room.

She held out an envelope. "The owner wanted me to give you this if ever you should come in here. I would have given this to you sooner, but I didn't recognize you. This is all I had to go by."

She pointed to the wall where a framed photograph hung. My hand flew to my lips as I held back a gasp. It was me. The same picture my mom had of me from when I was young and she made me get dressed up for pictures in the park.

I blinked at the photograph. "Why am I on the wall?"

"It's Jack," she said as if it was obvious.

I shook my head. "No, that's me." I pointed to the little girl in the center of the picture.

"Yes, but there . . ." She pointed to a man in the distance who was waving at the camera. "That's Jack."

Tears stung my eyes. It was Jack Franklin. My father. I had a photograph of my father all this time. He saw me that day.

That was why I was dressed up. I wasn't there to just take pretty pictures on a beautiful spring day; I was there to meet my father.

"I don't—" The words caught in my throat. "I don't remember meeting him . . .."

"Well, he remembered meeting you. He went on and on about how beautiful and smart you were. He was so proud of you."

My eyes slid to the side as I watched the waitress gaze up at the picture. She was smiling.

That was when it sank into my overwhelmed brain: Jack Franklin owned Jack's Place. He was Jack.

"You knew him, then?"

"Yes. He didn't come in often, but when he did, he always brought gifts and wild tales of his travels. He traveled a lot. And to think, that's what killed him." She shook her head, the light dimming from her eyes.

I wanted to ask her a million questions about him. But as I opened my mouth, a thought bubbled up inside.

Why hadn't he visited me?

And that question released the years of anger pent-up inside.

"I'm his daughter, you know."

"Really? He never said. Just thought you were his niece or family friend. He never mentioned a daughter."

My jaw tightened. "Yeah, I didn't find out until recently. Not even that day. For such a nice guy, he didn't really care about me, did he?"

"No, that's not true," she said, but I saw what was behind her eyes. Confusion. Questions.

My version of Jack Franklin didn't match her version. His own flesh and blood was forgettable to him, but employees were worth his time and gifts.

I wasn't mad at her; she hadn't known. But if I stayed here with her in the hallway asking questions, I'd end up yelling at her, and she didn't deserve that.

I turned, heading back toward the swinging green doors. "Thanks for this." I waved the envelope in the air, refusing to glance back.

"Anything you want, it's on the house," she said, trying to make up for years of neglect from a man who lied to us all.

Knight stared at me as I made my way back to the table. The others were too busy stuffing their faces. I even heard a moan come from Caleb. They were lost in diner food heaven.

"What was that all about?" Knight asked.

"Just realizing how much my father wanted nothing to do with me." I glanced down at the envelope as I scooted into the booth. Knight shifted to let me take his place.

Whatever that man had to say to me in the letter, he had years to tell me. I tightened my fingers and balled up the envelope, tossing it to the ground. Knight watched me with concern etching his brow but said nothing.

Fuck my father.

TEN

Violet

THE LIGHT STREAMED INTO Knight's room, and I turned my head to watch the blackout shade automatically rise.

Knight shifted, his arm still draped over my naked stomach. As he moved, he tightened his hold on me. If I had wanted to get up, I couldn't.

It was Sunday morning, the day after the bus driver's body had been found. Everyone got alerts on their phones that school would be canceled the upcoming week because of a concerning development. That was how Green Hills Academy labeled the death.

A concerning development . . .

I almost laughed when I read it. I never would have called a body in cement a concerning development. A tragedy, yes. Disturbing, absolutely.

Knight's finger drew tiny circles around my belly button, and warmth bloomed between my legs like a Pavlovian response. He did that the few times we slept in each other's beds, and I knew what came next. Me.

"I love waking up to your sweet pussy in the morning." His rough voice vibrated in my ear.

His fingers slid down until those circles he made were swirling around my clit. My nipples hardened, and I couldn't wait to feel his cock rocking inside me.

I arched my back, my ass grinding against his hardening cock. He hissed. The hand that had worked my clit stopped to grab my hips, pulling me over his cock.

I was about to get what I wanted.

"Everything about you, Violet, is luscious."

And everything about him was dark and sexy and heartbreakingly addictive.

I knew the drill. Reaching forward to the bedside table, I grabbed a condom and handed it over to him. Within seconds, I heard the rip of the wrapper and knew he was rolling it on. Once he rubbed the head of his cock to my core, I bit my lip with anticipation.

Knight didn't hesitate as he rocked inside me. I lifted my leg, angling it so he could go deeper.

"Fuck, Violet. I'll never get used to how good you feel." His fingers slid back to my clit, causing my core to clench.

"Don't stop," I murmured as I gasped for breath.

His fingers stilled and moved away, and I whimpered. He was messing with me. I knew what he wanted, but I wanted control for once. I wasn't about to give in so easily.

"Violet." My name on his lips was a command.

My hand slipped down my stomach. I didn't need him. My clit didn't care whose finger rubbed it to oblivion, just that it got there.

Before I could reach my swollen nub, Knight grabbed my wrist. My lips curled into a smile. Apparently neither of us would get what we wanted this morning.

"Is this a game to you?" he whispered in my ear.

"We're just fucking. Relax." I would have rolled my eyes too, but his cock was making it hard for me to be annoyed.

Knight must've known, so he stopped. He slid out of me and rolled me onto my back, pinning my arms over my head.

"Is that what we're doing? Just fucking." His molten eyes gazed at my lips before traveling to my tits.

"Isn't it? What we have isn't romance. We're not even boyfriend and girlfriend."

I swallowed, my heart pounding my chest. Why did I care so much how he answered? I didn't trust the guy, so why was I terrified he would agree to everything I just said?

His nose flared, and then he turned his

head. Was he about to get up? Leave me unsatisfied?

When he turned his head back, there was hurt in his eyes. It was clear that whatever wall Knight had erected had just fallen.

"I consider you my girlfriend, Violet."

"Oh," I said like an idiot.

The guy just called me his girl, and that was all I could come up with? Wow. I realized I was the asshole at the moment.

He gave a hard laugh. "I guess I was wrong then."

Knight let go of my arms and sat up on his heels.

"No, that came out wrong. I just . . ." I lifted onto my elbows. "I thought you didn't see me like that."

I thought, after all that had happened to him, he wasn't the type of guy to have a girlfriend.

"I bailed you out of jail. I had you move in with me to protect you. I got you out of Seraphina's basement. Why would I do all that for some girl I just wanted to fuck occasionally?"

I frowned. "Well, when you put it like that . . . I'd like to be your girlfriend."

His brows went up. "Then you'll do as I say."

My cheeks flamed. "Okay."

His gaze rested on my tits as he demanded, "Lie down and hook your knees over your elbows. Open wide for me."

I already felt myself dripping down my thigh at his command. I did as he requested. He stared at my pussy for a moment, which only caused me to squirm. I wanted him to touch me. Lick me. Do something.

The only thing I felt was the cool air

against my throbbing clit.

He tugged on his ball sack as he watched me.

"Knight. Please." I arched my back, wanting anything the boy gave me.

But the gesture brought nothing but an unsatisfying smirk from his lips. After a moment, he got off the bed.

I stared at him in shock. "What the hell?"

I did as he asked, even begged, but that wasn't enough.

He walked around the bed and grabbed something from his desk drawer—the drawer that was locked. He palmed the item so I couldn't see what it was as he walked back to the bed. Knight nestled between my legs again. I lifted my head to glimpse what he had, but he hid it well.

A soft buzzing sound started, and then

I felt it. My clit jerked, and I groaned as I felt the vibration across my soaked pussy lips.

It was barely anything, but even with that small tease, I wanted more.

My toes curled as Knight tested the vibrator's effects on me. Each time it touched me, I jolted, and warm heat bloomed from my core.

He slipped it inside. It wasn't big, more the size of his finger, but the vibrating had me panting. As quickly as he pushed it into my core, he removed it.

"Knight, please. I need more."

His eyes flickered up to me. "What you need to do is take what I give you."

I would have been furious if this had been anyone else in any other situation. But it was Knight, and my body gobbled up every nasty word he said to me as if only his voice had the power to make me come.

I groaned and arched my back. My body was on fire. I had never wanted to be fucked so badly in my life.

He lifted the vibrator, let it slide over my thigh, just out of reach of my pussy. I shifted my hips, wanting to inch closer.

"You're so greedy, Violet. And your pussy . . . it keeps dripping, begging for me."

"Yes," I said with a gasp.

I was ready to burst.

He let it touch me once more, and my mouth fell open without a sound. Knight moved it down until it circled my puckered hole.

"I think it fits better in here," Knight said as he wiggled the vibrator inside my asshole.

My core clenched, and I knew it wouldn't be long before I came. I just needed something else. His fingers flicking my clit or his cock grinding into my core, a little extra to send me over.

He lowered himself until I felt his hot breath on my core. I reached for his head to push him closer, but he knew what I would do. His hands went up and grabbed mine, pinning them to the bed.

Then I felt it. His tongue reached out and swiped my clit. My teeth gnashed together as I arched my back.

I only had time to call out his name before I fell over the peak into oblivion. My orgasm was all-consuming, and I hadn't noticed he had adjusted his position until he hovered over me.

Knight wasn't gentle as he pushed his cock inside me. He placed his hands on either side of my head and closed his eyes, pausing for a moment. I couldn't make a sound as the movement of his cock sent my climax soaring once again.

With a breath, he moved his hips, slowly at first, but once he opened his eyes and looked down at me, his rhythm picked up pace.

I wrapped my arms around him, my fingers digging into his back. His eyes bore into mine as what I felt blurred into wave after wave of orgasms shredding me.

"You're mine. Always," Knight said, his voice ragged.

"Yes." I didn't hesitate.

If it meant sex like this, then I'd tell him yes a thousand times if he asked me to.

"No more just fucking. My cock was made for your pussy." As if his words weren't enough of a reminder of how much my body craved his, he reached over and pinched my nipple.

"Yes, Knight. Fuck, yes."

His hips shifted, and the rocking grew less steady. It wasn't long before he buried his head into my shoulder and called out my name.

I cradled him in my arms as his back moved up and down with rapid breaths. It was a few moments before my body sank back to reality.

But my ass kept vibrating.

I tapped his shoulder. "Hey, can you take the vibrator out?"

He lifted onto his elbows and chuckled. "What? You don't want to walk around with a vibrating ass all day?"

I pursed my lips and pushed him off me, rolling onto my stomach.

He reached down, and the vibration stopped. After a moment, he removed the vibrator. I watched him walk over to his desk and toss it into the trash.

I lifted onto my elbow, leaning my

head on my hand. "You're throwing it away? But I liked it."

"It's used. I have more." Knight walked over and crawled back into bed with me. "Nothing used will ever touch your body."

Seemed wasteful to me. Sex toys weren't cheap. But Knight was a billionaire, so I guessed he could afford to toss sex toys away like candy wrappers.

"I'm pretty sure used stuff touches my body all the time."

He rested his head on his hand and scooted closer. "Like what?" His finger traced around my nipple, causing it to harden.

"My clothes, for one thing."

Even when my mom and I originally got my clothes, they were used. Thrift store and Salvation Army items were staples of the Adler wardrobe.

He rolled onto his back, pulling me to

his side. Now it was my turn to trace my finger along his nipple.

"Not anymore."

"What do you mean, not anymore?"

His finger slid under my chin, and he tilted my head up to meet his gaze. "I mean, I'm buying you all new clothes."

"Knight, that's sweet, but I really don't need—"

"I told you, what you need is to take what I give you." His finger slipped from my chin and tucked some hair behind my ear.

I should have told him no, but a little thrill wiggled its way inside my chest. My cheeks heated, as did my core.

God help me, I enjoyed what he was doing. I felt cherished, spoiled, and when he became demanding, I nearly creamed myself.

I had spent my entire life taking care

of my mom and making sure I survived. Was it wrong to want this sexy billionaire to spoil me?

ELEVEN

Violet

"I WANT TO SEE that one," Knight ordered, pointing to the black cashmere cocktail dress.

"Of course, Mr. King. Perhaps the lady would like to look at something from our brand-new spring line, not just the fall line? I got the spring line yesterday. You'd be the first to see it." The saleswoman's eyes bounced between me and Knight, unable to decipher which of us made the decisions.

Knight turned his head, his arm slung over my shoulders as we sat on the velvet couch in the private viewing room of a boutique on Main Drive.

"Would you like that?" he whispered in my ear.

A shiver ran down my neck.

Ever since we agreed to be boyfriend and girlfriend earlier this morning, Knight had been different. More controlling. More determined. And so much sexier.

I lifted my gaze to the woman, worried she'd be uncomfortable with Knight acting this way. Since we arrived, he hadn't stopped touching me.

But the woman smiled politely, as if his controlling behavior was totally normal.

She cleared her throat. "Let me add

that each piece is individually made. One of a kind. No one else would have it."

His hand lifted to my throat. My nipples turned to spikes as his fingers trailed a line up my neck and he hooked my chin, turning me to face him.

"Anything you want," he said, staring at my lips.

"Yes," I squeaked out.

Knight turned to the woman. "Show it to us."

She nodded and scurried off.

The same thing had happened when I went shopping with Arabella at the mall. Models came out with clothes on for me to choose from. I tried to focus on what they were wearing, but Knight kept tracing circles just under my earlobe.

My pulse quickened. Glancing over at Knight, he stared at the models as if they were advertisements interrupting his favorite show—like they were something to be tolerated.

"Can I try on the clothes?" I asked the saleswoman.

Her brown eyes widened. "Of course. If that's what you wish."

"What a perfect idea. Everyone out." Knight waved his hand.

All the models scurried out of the room as the saleswoman pushed over a rack filled with clothes in various shades and styles—ranging from casual and flirty to formal and demure. Knight stared at the woman until she left.

Once the door was closed, he said, "Take off your clothes."

My clit pulsed. I stood and immediately started to remove my clothing. It wasn't long before I stood in front of him completely naked.

Knight still sat on the couch. His gaze traveled up my body, and it felt like a hot knife slicing through butter.

"Go over to the mirror." He flicked his finger and pointed behind him.

I glanced over at the clothes. I guessed he was going to bring over what he wanted me to wear.

Only he didn't. Knight strolled over, his gaze glued to my reflection until he stopped behind me. With a jolt, his hand landed on my ass.

"Fuck, you are gorgeous."

He slipped his hand down until his fingers brushed over my folds.

"I knew you were wet, just itching for me to fuck you." His nose flared as he pushed a few fingers inside me.

I groaned and placed my hand on the wall, next to the mirror, to hold myself up.

He used his other hand to unzip his jeans and pull his cock out. "You see how hard you make me?"

I licked my lips. "Yes."

"You want this? Want me to bury it deep inside you?"

I nodded as my knees trembled.

His jaw tightened. He slid his hand out

from inside me and dug into his pocket. In less than a minute, he had a condom on.

"God, I love your pussy." His eyes held a longing I hadn't seen before. And for a moment, I wondered if he really was talking about my pussy or more than that.

I shook my head as he stepped behind me. We had grown closer over the last two months, and I knew he wanted me more than for just a good fuck. But the way he stared at me made me worry that he wanted something more than I was prepared to give.

I'd let him fuck me, use my body anytime and anywhere, but not my heart.

Never my heart.

I bent my head to the side. "Then what's stopping you from taking it?"

The corner of his mouth curved. Knight's hand eased over my back, guiding me to bend over.

It reminded me of our first time when he bent me over in the woods. I never thought sex could be like that—raw, dirty, and mind-blowing.

There was no dirt beneath my feet or mud to soil my clothes now, just perfumed air and classical music to muffle my cries.

I steadied myself with my hands against the wall as Knight placed the tip of his cock at my apex.

"Only you can stop me, Violet." His brow rose, and something in his voice made me swallow. "What I do to you, you're going to want to scream. Don't." That was his only warning before he slammed into me.

He was right. My eyes widened, and my mouth fell open, but I held back my scream. He filled me, and all thoughts of hearts and feelings evaporated.

Knight's hand slid up my back. I winced as he pulled my hair. Lifting my head, I saw darkening gray eyes staring at me through the mirror.

"Watch what I do to you," he said as he

pumped into me.

What I saw was a girl barely able to hold on. My tits bounced as my hips rippled from Knight's pounding action. My core tightened as he fucked me.

The veins in his arms and neck grew. With the mirror, I saw it all. Not just the drops of sweat glistening on his brow or the flush that took over my chest, but things I had never noticed before.

Like how he softly rubbed my back like his hands needed to caress me at all times. He was controlling, dirty, but also caring.

He wanted me to see what he did to me, and I saw it for the first time.

I didn't want to witness this. I wanted the devil. The devil who took and left me weak and wanting. I was used to that.

He brought me here today to give me everything, including his heart.

His eyes flickered to mine. "Do you see?"

"Yes."

I wanted to lie. I wanted to tell him no. Maybe he would pull my hair or pinch my nipples, something to remind me of the pain he easily gave me.

But I couldn't lie to him. Too many people who were supposed to care for him had lied. And I knew all too well how that felt.

He bent over my back, dotting kisses along my spine. I heard him inhale, and my eyes warmed with unshed tears.

Knight was never the devil. He was just a broken boy who needed someone to help pick up the pieces of his heart.

"Why can't we stay like this forever?" he whispered against my back.

His rhythm shifted and slowed. Perhaps to make it last.

I smiled. "I'm pretty sure they'd kick us out."

I needed to break this, lighten it up. If I couldn't bring out the devil, perhaps I could make him laugh. Forget about his heart and how I affected it.

"Not if I paid them enough." His hand drifted between my thighs. Knight slowly strummed my clit like a distracted guitarist on a lazy afternoon.

But it didn't distract me—it intensified *everything*.

"Knight," I moaned.

He looked over at me in the mirror and grinned. The devil was back.

His other hand reached around and rubbed my nipple between his thumb and forefinger. My core tightened, and I knew he felt it. Knight groaned, but he didn't let up.

I pushed back into him, seeking more.

But it wasn't necessary because only moments later, I came.

His hand left my tit and wrapped over my mouth. It was a good thing because my release was intense, and I had forgotten to keep quiet.

After a minute, Knight pushed deep inside me a few times before he stopped.

Knight wasn't moving. He was inside me, and my legs were turning to jelly. Thankfully, his arm slid around my torso and held me tight.

"It's never a dull moment with you." His voice was rough but full of humor.

"You're the one who told me to get naked."

He kissed my back and stood, holding on to my hips as he slid out of me. I leaned against the wall as I stepped away, and he removed the condom. There was a box of tissues on a round table in the corner, which he made use of and discarded the condom in the wastebasket once he was done.

Instead of getting dressed, he looked over the rack of clothes. Reaching in, he pulled a few things out.

Knight came over and pushed them at me—a pair of jeans and the softest sweater

I had ever felt. "You can wear these home. Everything else we'll take, too. Whatever you don't like, we'll send back. Now get dressed; I have to take you shoe shopping next."

I stood there staring at him, my mouth hanging open as he got dressed.

He couldn't be serious. All those clothes must cost more than what my aunt made in a year.

"The entire spring line?"

I had no idea why I asked that. I guessed I was in too much shock. Maybe he meant what he just told me to wear.

He ignored me, and I made sure I had my clothes on when he went to the door and opened it.

My cheeks warmed as the saleswoman showed up within seconds. The place smelled like sex, and if she was that close, surely she heard us.

"Have you decided?" she asked with her perfectly neutral, non-judging smile.

"Yes, we'll take both lines. The fall and spring line."

"Holy shit," I blurted out.

Knight's eyes shot to me with a warning in his gaze before he turned back to the woman.

I stood there dumbfounded while he handed over his card. The entire transaction took less than a minute.

Once he was leading me out of the store, I glanced around. "Where are all the clothes?"

He slid his hand into mine as we strolled down the picturesque street. There were planters filled with fall shrubbery and pumpkins framing every colorful shop door. The sidewalk was practically gleaming, and there were no cracks in the cement. Everything around here looked as if the town spent a lot of money for upkeep.

Not at all like the south side.

"They are being wrapped up and

delivered to the house. Are you hungry, or would you like to look at shoes?"

I stopped and glanced around. What was this? It was like something from a fairytale. I was Cinderella, and he was a really devilish Prince Charming. And with the surrounding pumpkins, I suspected a carriage would appear at any moment.

"Maybe we eat first, then shoe shopping," I said as a smile broke out over my face.

All this was new and so different, but that didn't matter. For once in my life, I wanted that princess dream to come true.

And here I was, standing in the middle of it.

Even if it all faded tomorrow, I would soak up the golden rays Knight was offering today. My life had been rough, and it was time I got my moment to enjoy these riches.

TWELVE

Violet

"HOLY SHIT. YOU WEREN'T kidding. Did he buy out the shop?" Arabella's eyes scanned my bedroom. She took in the four different clothing racks that were parked in the middle of my room.

"Yes."

I was next to one rack, petting a velvet dress that I planned to wear to whatever winter party came up.

No more hanging out in my pajamas watching movies. This girl had a wardrobe, and she wasn't about to hide it.

Her hazel eyes snapped over to me. "Really? Like completely bought out an entire store?"

I sighed and grinned like a fool. "One hundred percent yes."

But he gave me orgasms first, though I left that part out. It was the perfect day. Every fantasy I ever had came true on Sunday.

"Damn, that boy must love you."

My grin faltered. "No . . . I don't think he loves me. Yes, we like each other, and you know . . ." I rolled my hand around.

"Sex. I think the word you're looking for is, you have sex with him." She used hand gestures too, but they were more on the crude side.

"Yes. Anyway, just because we do that, and he bought me some clothes—"

"*Some clothes?*" She spun around with her arms in the air. "These are much more than *some clothes*. You can start your own boutique inside your bedroom."

"The guy's a billionaire. To him, it's just some clothes."

She came over to me and grabbed my hand. "And the sex? Is it just some sex, or is it making *lurve?*" She made kissing noises.

I pulled my hand back and folded my arms. "Are you seriously being this immature right now?"

"Yes. Because it's fun to watch you turn all red." She bopped my nose with her finger and turned back to the clothing racks.

"Speaking of Mr. Moneybags, will he be joining us in the hot tub?"

It was Monday, and since we didn't have school because of that bus driver found in the basement, I had invited Arabella over for a dip in the hot tub.

"No. He's hanging out at Caleb's today."

"I didn't even know there was a hot tub here."

"Neither did—" I stopped myself before I said too much. "I mean, I hadn't realized it until Knight showed me last night.

It was too late. Arabella instantly figured out what I was trying to hide.

"And by showed you, you mean you two fooled around in it."

I wrinkled my nose. "No."

We made out in it, but it wasn't until we got out of the hot tub that he bent me over and fucked me. Technically, nothing actually happened inside the hot tub.

She pursed her lips and stared at me for a moment before she shook her head and said, "Sure. I totally believe you."

I rolled my eyes and went over to a

rack, pulling out a bathing suit. "I got a few suits and wanted to try out one of them."

"Oh, you didn't try one out last night?"

My eyes widened, and I stammered, trying to say something.

"That would be a no, then. You and Knight sat in the hot tub naked last night and didn't have sex. Like I said, I totally believe you."

"Let's just get into our suits and head downstairs."

She pointed to my window. "Why don't we get ready in the pool house? That's what it's there for."

I bit my lip. "Maybe, uh . . ."

"Oh shit, I totally forgot. We can just change here. No big deal." She shook her head.

I hadn't stepped foot inside the pool house since I left it the day the mayor and his friends tried to rape me. Sometimes I didn't even want to look out my bedroom window because I knew I would see the pool house.

It was weird. I had my good days when I could walk out on the deck or, like last night, walk by it on my way to the hot tub, and it would barely register. But then, I had moments like this, when even the thought made my skin crawl.

I took a deep breath and let it out. "No, we can go to the pool house. It's been two months. I need to get over it. Right?"

She shook her head and came over to me. Placing her hands on my upper arms, her touch gentle, she said, "Violet, however long it takes is however long it takes. I would be surprised if you were over it already. What you described sounded scary as shit. If you don't even want to go out there, we can stay in and watch that new zombie series I've been hearing about."

Fuck. I hated that I was ruining what could be an amazing day. The mayor wasn't in that pool house; I wouldn't be going in there alone. Yet, I could feel the sweat on my palms as I thought about stepping foot inside that place.

My eyes searched the room. "All these clothes . . . they were meant for a girl who didn't let memories frighten her," I whispered.

"These clothes were meant for *you*. You're the strongest, most badass girl I know. You stood up to Seraphina when no one else did, and you took on the devil. The two people everyone at school feared, you took them both down in less than two months."

If I was so badass, then why was I letting a memory frighten me?

I shrugged. "Seraphina was easy. She just needed someone who didn't take her shit."

"And Knight?"

I smirked. "What can I say? This pussy is golden."

Arabella's head fell back as a roar of

laughter came out. My face was red. I couldn't believe I just said that, but I smiled nonetheless.

"It must be," she commented in between chuckles.

It was nice to laugh with a friend. After all that had happened to me over the past two months, I always had Arabella.

Pushing up my chin, I said, "Let's go."

"Go where?"

"The pool house."

Her brows rose, and she took a step back, her eyes searching mine. "You sure?"

"Yeah. I may get there, immediately change my mind and suddenly need to watch zombies. But I at least want to try."

She nodded and came over, throwing her arm around my shoulder. "Okay. I'll be at your side the entire time."

Arabella did as promised. We grabbed her suit from her car and headed to the pool house. It surprised me when we got to the door that whatever fear I had up in my room had disappeared.

I was tense, but that was because I worried at any moment I'd panic. I'd see something, or a smell would trigger a memory and send me running.

But as we opened the door and stepped inside, nothing happened. The only smell was dust—I noticed a fine film of it coated everything. There were footprints too. Someone had been in here recently, probably Knight or one of his servants.

"Are you okay?" Arabella asked as we reached the living room—the same room the mayor and his friends held me down in.

"Yeah, I think so." I took a breath and let out a laugh. "I think the dust helps. It just feels old and forgotten. Like something from long ago."

"If you think you're okay, then I'll head to the bedroom in the back and change." She stared at me, waiting for my response.

I nodded. "Go. I'll check the fridge. If I

remember correctly, I think there's some bottled water left in there."

She headed down the hallway and called out, "Also chips. Anything salty."

"How about some melty chocolate-covered pretzels?" I called out, holding back my laughter.

"You're gross," she said before I heard the door to the bedroom slam.

I chuckled and made my way into the small kitchen. I glanced at the granite counter and frowned. Something had spilled on it, probably from the last time I was here, and now it had darkened and congealed.

"Yuck."

I grabbed the door to the refrigerator and pulled. When it opened, a putrid smell hit my nostrils instantly. It was so intense, I closed my eyes and covered my face.

"Oh, shit." I could taste it. "What the fuck?"

I blinked, and what I was looking at

didn't register for a second. I tilted my head, trying to piece together the puzzle of what was inside the fridge.

But after a few seconds, it came to me. My mouth fell open as I tried to scream, but horror clawed at my voice, and nothing came out.

I stumbled back, grabbing at the counter, and my fingers pressed into that congealed spill. I lifted my fingers and realized that spill came from what was inside the refrigerator.

"What the hell, Violet? Did you fart?" Arabella's voice came from the hallway.

I turned and moved to the doorway to stop her from coming inside the kitchen, but it was too late.

She rounded the corner and covered her nose. "God, what's that—"

Her gaze traveled to the fridge, and that was when she stopped. She was frozen, staring at Crystal Hillingham's chopped-up body that was shoved inside the refrigerator.

THIRTEEN

Knight

"**AND WHEN WAS THE** last time you went into the pool house, Mr. King?" the detective asked me.

It was a cool autumn day, and the sun was bright in the clear blue sky. I wore my sunglasses as I stood by the pool and watched as police swarmed the area. Only a few people were allowed inside the pool house, and they had to wear gloves and coverings on their feet.

The detective's brown eyes slid to the other side of the pool. And I knew why.

Violet was seated on one of the pool chairs. She had found Crystal's body. Well. . . pieces of it.

She had texted me there was an emergency and to come home. My stomach bottomed out when I arrived and saw what the emergency was.

"Just before you arrived. My girlfriend texted me, and when I got home, I had to see it for myself."

"And that's when you," he lifted a previous page of notes on the notepad in his hand, "ran to the bathroom and puked?"

I nodded. I still felt queasy.

"When was the last time you saw the deceased?"

I blinked, unsure if I should tell him the truth. I lowered my gaze to his notepad. Was he working for my uncle?

"About a week and a half ago at her Pumpkin Luncheon."

"So, we can verify you were at the party?"

Shit. After what Crystal was going to do to Violet, I was glad she was dead. But I never wanted such a gruesome end for her, no matter how much I hated the woman.

But if I explained why I was there, it would make both Violet and me look guilty.

My nose flared. *That's exactly what my uncle wanted.* That piece of shit must have killed Crystal and purposely placed her body to make it seem like we did it.

"I wasn't really at the party. I was in the basement. Along with my uncle, the mayor."

The detective's suspicious expression

faded into one of shock. "The mayor was in the basement of the Pumpkin Luncheon? Why was he there?"

I was tired of my uncle's control on me and the people he loved. We all walked on glass, fearing what he might do next. Maybe this guy was on my uncle's payroll, and if he was, it was time for me to send a message to my not-so-loving uncle.

"I suspect he was there to *take care* of his problem."

The detective narrowed his eyes. "Take care?"

"I'm sure you know by now that my uncle, the mayor . . ." I pointed to his notepad. "You might want to jot this down."

He nodded as I snapped him out of his surprised state. "Yes, of course."

"The mayor had a plan. It involved making lots of money on a now defunct cancer drug. It serves some purpose, or he wouldn't have invested lots of money in it.

Crystal invested in the non-working drug as well."

"But why?"

I snapped my fingers. "That is the question. I suspect my uncle had something to do with Crystal's death. Maybe she threatened him, or maybe she did something he didn't want her to do, or maybe he knew this drug was going to make him so much money that he kept it all to himself. I just don't know yet. Maybe you can help me with that, you know, since you're a detective."

I left out the part where I knew the drug was being turned into the street drug Elicit. *Let him work that part out himself. It's what he's paid for.*

The guy coughed unconvincingly. "My job is to work this case, not deal with the beef you have with your uncle, Mr. King."

I scratched the back of my head and glanced over at Violet. Arabella was sitting next to her, and they were both drinking from mugs. Coffee, I suspected. I noticed Violet's mug shook in her hands.

Anger spiked in my veins.

"Funny, but I thought your job was to catch criminals. Yet, my uncle still walks free." My eyes swung back to his.

"You think your uncle did this?" He threw a thumb over his shoulder back toward the pool house.

"Considering when my uncle arrived, he went straight to the basement and looked at Crystal Hillingham's unconscious body on the floor like it was a bug about to be squashed. And she never showed up at her own party; not even her daughter knew where she went. Yes, I believe my uncle had something to do with her murder."

The cop glared at me for only a moment before he stepped closer. He leaned in and whispered, "There are some people here who won't say a nasty word about the mayor. They'll say any suspicions are just rumors, and any evidence that arises involving the mayor has been tampered with."

"Yeah, I know the cops have been bought by my uncle."

"Not all of us, though. If what you say is true, then I'll pass it along to the people who matter. You understand?"

I nodded. Maybe there was hope that my uncle could be brought down.

"But until then, I'm going to ask you to tamp down your accusations about him. I don't want anyone getting suspicious."

"Yes, I get it."

His eyes flickered to where Violet sat. "Watch out for her. I overheard some cops mention her name. I suspect the mayor will do something to her . . . and it won't be good. The body showing up in the pool house might have been a warning."

He was right. The fact that Violet used to live in that pool house, and it was where my uncle had last seen her, was a little too much of a coincidence.

Bodies were piling up, and Violet had been in each of their lives—the bus driver, John Lenker, and now Crystal. Each of them played a part in something terrible that happened to her, and each of them died in a very gruesome way.

Either my uncle was punishing them—which would mean he cared for Violet. But that man wouldn't care about his own reflection unless it could get him money.

Or he was framing her. She would have motive to hurt each one of those people. The police would discover that, if they hadn't already.

Then she'd become a suspect. A prime suspect.

"Thanks." I nodded at the detective and went over to Violet.

I sat on the edge of her lounge chair and rubbed her back. "How are you doing?"

"That smell," she murmured. "I can't

seem to get it out of my nose. I thought the coffee would drown it out, but it's not working." Violet lifted her mug.

"It was disgusting," Arabella added.

"I wonder how long she's been here?" I asked, knowing full well neither of them had the answer.

"Long enough for the smell to build up, but not long enough for it to leak out of the fridge and stink up the pool house," Arabella said before taking a sip from her mug.

"I guess we'll find out soon. Once the medical examiner does their job."

"We saw footprints," Violet said, staring at the ground.

"Really?"

"Yeah, there was a lot of dust on the floor, and there were footprints when we walked inside. I told the police about it."

I pursed my lips. Much good that would do. I was sure they wouldn't do a thing about the footprints.

"That was probably the person who put the body in the refrigerator," I said.

I was about to suggest we move inside the house when my phone vibrated in my pocket.

When I lifted it out, I saw it was a text from Edwin. An icy shiver ran down my spine.

"What is it?" Violet looked over at my phone.

"Uh, it's Edwin. Seems they have dropped the charges for murder against him." I glanced up at Violet. "The police have a new suspect."

Both Violet and Arabella grinned.

"That's great," Violet said as she placed a hand on my arm.

Sure, I was glad my friend was free and clear, but I worried about who was taking his place.

"Violet . . . why don't we go inside?"

This was a problem that needed a solution, and I couldn't let on to anyone how I was about to solve it.

FOURTEEN

Violet

THIS PLACE WAS AS dusty as the pool house.

My stomach flipped. Just the thought of the pool house made me want to retch.

It had been two days since I found Crystal's body in that refrigerator. And since then, I'd been hiding out here, in the attic.

I hated it up here. Knight had provided me with a mattress and things to entertain myself, but I felt like some kind of kept woman. Not allowed to appear in public, and here only for his pleasure. He allowed me to go down to my room to shower, but I had to eat in the attic.

I would have left by now, but once he told me what he suspected his uncle was up to, I knew I had to hide out.

Knight kept me company as much as possible. But even our talks and fooling around weren't enough to make me happy. I never thought I would crave fresh air and sunlight in my life.

Now I understood how people got cabin fever.

"It's happened." Knight's voice came from behind me, causing me to gasp.

"What's happened?"

He moved closer because, even with

the lamp he brought up yesterday, most of the place was dark.

Knight held up his phone as if I could tell what was on it.

"You're wanted in connection to the murders of John Lenker, Trey Webb, and Crystal Hillingham."

I swallowed and suddenly felt hot. My mind raced to ways I could explain that I had nothing to do with their deaths.

"Who's Trey Webb?" I asked. I had never heard of him.

"The bus driver."

"Oh, right. Never really knew his name."

Knight came over to my side where I was seated on the mattress. He slid his arms around me, pulling me in for a hug. As wonderful as he felt, nothing would soothe me now.

"It's all over. Your uncle threatened me. In the first note I got from him, it said how he was going to destroy me. Well, he did it. I'll probably spend the rest of my life in jail for crimes I didn't commit."

"Hey." Knight pulled back and looked deep into my eyes. "That will not happen, I promise. He's the one who committed those crimes, not you. He'll pay for them."

My lips thinned. "You sure about that? You know for a fact that Ichabod King killed those three people?"

"No." He sighed. "Not yet. But I think I may have a few leads."

I groaned and threw my head into my hands. "That's all we ever have. Anytime we get information, it only leads to more questions. I feel like your uncle wove a web so complicated, we'll never be able to unravel it."

I felt lost. Once Knight and his friends rescued me from Crystal's basement, I thought all the awful stuff was over. But I was wrong. It was only the beginning.

"I ran into my uncle as I was leaving Crystal's basement."

I turned on the mattress to face him. "What? Why didn't you say anything?"

"I didn't want to scare you, but since you found Crystal's body, I don't think there's anything that can scare you anymore."

I don't know about that. His uncle's doing a good job of keeping me on edge.

"The necklace I gave you to wear to the luncheon . . . it had a listening device."

"I know. We fought about it while trying to escape the basement, remember?"

He nodded. "Yes, I do. But the necklace fell and was left in the room they trapped you in."

"I am sorry about that. I know it was your mom's and—"

He waved a hand and cut me off. "I have lots of my mom's jewelry. It's not as if that's the piece I kept close to my heart. This is what I keep close to remind me of her." He reached under his shirt collar and pulled out the cross necklace he used to break into the basement of Green Hills Academy.

"That was hers?"

"Yeah. I'm not religious, but she was. I thought if I wore it . . . I don't know. I feel close to her when I wear this."

I clasped his hand in mine. "I understand. I'm sure your mom would love that you wear it."

We sat for a moment in silence before he said, "I saw the necklace in that basement room, but I left it there."

I tilted my head. "Why?"

"To record my uncle. I collected all that I recorded and everything I downloaded from the bus driver's phone, and then I gave it to a journalist. If anything happens to me, she'll have that information. She also has some things she gathered herself that can bring him down, evidence that he used to bribe the plane mechanic."

"Okay, but that doesn't help me right now. How do I get out of here?"

He took a breath, as if steeling himself for something.

"Please don't be mad. But that letter Jack Franklin left you . . . the one you balled up and tossed aside at the diner this past weekend . . . well, I kept it."

I sat there, quiet. My father never lent a hand to help me. I picked at the jewels on my bracelet. The one I was only supposed to get on my eighteenth birthday, but because of a clerical error, I got it on my sixteenth. The only thing he gave me that was worth anything.

Knight took the letter out of his back pocket and held it up. The light filled the smooth surfaces, and the shadows intensified the wrinkles from when I balled it up.

At any time, Jack could have sent that to me, but he left it at the diner in case I might show up. How lazy was that? He couldn't even be bothered to mail the thing.

"I threw it away for a reason, Knight."

"I know, but maybe there's something in here that could help us. Help you."

I didn't know if I was angry at my father for being such a deadbeat or that Knight was right. The only power I had against the mayor was that I was Jack Franklin's daughter.

Maybe there was a check in there that could pay for my legal fees. Something like that would help. It would be the absolute least his greedy ass could have done.

I plucked it from Knight's fingers and pushed the envelope around in my fingers.

"Do you want me to give you some privacy?"

"No. I want you to witness what a horrible man Jack Franklin was. My mom may have made excuses for him and loved him, but she must have been blinded by his charm or wealth or something."

I was grasping at anything, something that would explain why my mom would hold out hope for a man who obviously wanted nothing to do with her. She got knocked up, and he walked away. That story was too cliché for words.

I tore at the envelope and pulled out three pieces of paper. A smaller, square piece of paper fell to the ground.

I reached down and picked it up.

"It's a picture," I mumbled.

It was a photograph of me being held by Jack Franklin, though "held" was a loose word. I was a baby, sleeping on his stomach. He was asleep too.

I narrowed my eyes and recognized what he was lying on. "That's my couch."

The same old, ratty couch that was in our trailer. But in the picture, it looked new. A tear slipped down my cheek as I realized my dad was part of my life. In the beginning, he was there.

I lifted the three pieces of paper and started reading. One had six numbers. The other was a personal note to me from him.

"If you're reading this, it means I'm dead." My eyes warmed, and I felt tears form. I knew he was dead, but something about his writing got to me. Did he realize he might be killed?

I kept reading. He explained how he had to keep his relationship with my mom a secret. That his family would have disowned him if he had married her.

"Another rich man clinging to his fortune," I bit out under my breath.

"Jack never struck me as someone who cared much for money."

My head popped up, and I blinked at Knight. "You knew him?"

He shrugged. "A little. My parents were friends with him. He came over for dinner sometimes. He always seemed nice and very down to earth."

"Well, he cared more about his family's money than he did my mom or me."

"Have you read the entire letter?"

I glanced back down and shook my head. "No. I'm about halfway through."

Knight rubbed my back gently. "Maybe this isn't the right time, but with all we've been through, I don't know when the right time will be . . .. I just want you to know, Violet, I love you."

I gasped as my heart pounded in my chest. My eyes darted around the room.

"I'm not expecting you to say it back. It's been a rough couple of days. But I thought you should know that there are people around you who love you. That I will do anything for you. And that's partly why I kept that letter. Your father may not have been there, but I think he cared about you. I wanted to give you a chance to find the truth for yourself."

Tears formed in my eyes, and I tried to

blink them away. He wrapped his arm around me, and we sat there in silence as the warmth from Knight mixed with what my father wrote me. I felt loved and lost all at the same time.

"Why don't you keep reading? I'm going to meet with someone in my office, and after I'm done, I'll bring you up some cookies."

I felt like a child because the thought of cookies made me smile. "Okay."

I wish my aunt was here. Another business trip. If she were here I bet she would know how to deal with all this mess.

He got up and disappeared into the darkness. I heard him climb down the ladder. After some time staring off into space, willing myself to keep going, I gazed back down at the letters.

"I need to know the truth, no matter how much it hurts," I said to myself.

I gasped as I continued to read the letter. What my father wrote surprised me, and not in a good way.

"I would have given it all up for Rose. For you, Violet. Walked away from my family's vast fortune because there's nothing more valuable than love. But then members of my family threatened your mother. One day I received a letter in the mail that threatened you and warned what would happen if I didn't walk away from you both.

"It nearly destroyed me to leave, but I feared what would happen if I didn't. I couldn't tell your mom, but she found out. I don't know how, but she did. Please don't be angry with her. The choices she made in life . . . I think she was hurting. Those decisions ruled her life terribly."

I was sure he was talking about her taking drugs. This letter wasn't about to instantly wipe away years of anger, but I understood a little more why my mother started doing drugs.

She was lonely and hurting; and dealing with a child alone wasn't easy.

Maybe that was why she told me about Winter River University. She wanted me to succeed despite the wealthy, powerful people who ripped her family apart.

"I attached the letter I received that threatened you. Whether you believe me or not, I wanted you to know that you may not be safe. If you feel you need help, go to my assistant, Janice Hartley, at Franklin First. She knows all about this.

"I may not have been with you every day of your life, but it never stopped me from loving you, my little flower."

My hand flew to my mouth as I held back a cry. I had been wrong, all this time. So very, very wrong.

I let my stupid emotions cloud my judgment. My mother was right, and I felt like the biggest jerk for cursing her. For the years of anger I felt for the both of them. I wasted so much energy on something that was never true.

The threatening letter.

I pushed my father's letter aside and glanced down at the piece of paper that left me without a father. The words that turned my mother to drugs and left me fending for myself.

A shiver ran down my spine. "Oh god, no."

My hands shook as I held it up, rereading it. I stood with the letter in hand and raced to the ladder. Knight needed to see this. I didn't care if anyone saw me; the letter was too important to waste another minute.

Once I was down and out of the secret passage, I made my way toward the stairs to the first floor. Damn, why did the house have to be so big?

My feet pounded the Italian marble floor to the doorway of Knight's office. The sliding double doors were slightly pushed open, and the voice I heard coming out of it caused my eyes to widen.

"This wasn't easy for me. He's my

husband," Kiki said.

I stilled as my hand hovered over the doorknob. Leaning closer, I could only see Knight leaning back in his chair, his hands clasped behind his head.

"Yeah, but he's an old monster. I'm the younger, hotter model." Knight smirked.

I shook my head as bile crept up my throat. This couldn't be. Knight wouldn't cheat on me with his uncle's wife, would he?

"I suppose you're right. The longer I'm with Ichabod, the more repugnant he becomes. It'll be nice to be around someone who's easy on the eyes," she said with a giggle.

Fuck. I was about to be sick.

FIFTEEN

Violet

I RAN.

I couldn't take listening to them anymore. Were they about to fuck while Knight thought I was hidden away in the attic?

That was some twisted shit.

And I was about to tell Knight that the note threatening my father had come from Ichabod King. My dad thought it was his family, but I recognized that thick paper, the font—everything was exactly the same as the notes I had received.

By the time I made it back into the attic, I was gasping for breath. I flopped down, face-first, onto the mattress. A plume of dust erupted and filled the air.

My mouth pushed open, and I forced out a scream, muffled by the mattress and blanket I fisted and pushed into my face.

"Fuck him," I growled, my voice raw.

Was sticking his cock inside that plastic bimbo his way of getting information about his uncle? Jesus, I knew Knight wasn't a saint, but that was low, even for him.

Why was I here?

Knight kept telling me it was to protect

me, but was it? Maybe it was to fuck with me. Some twisted shit only a broken boy thought would be appealing.

I was his pretty doll he hid from the world while he taunted me with safety.

Not only was Kiki a phony plastic Barbie, but she was the enemy. I remembered how she treated me that first day I met her. She played the concerned caregiver for the camera perfectly, but once she was alone with me and the mayor, her fangs appeared.

I took a deep breath and decided. I could stay here and wonder what was in store for me. Sleep with one eye open in case Knight came for me in the dark.

Or, I could do what Adler women had always done—we take care of ourselves.

I stood from the mattress and glanced around. The only thing of mine here was my bracelet and my father's letter. I gathered what he wrote me, along with the photograph, and looked for my backpack.

It was in my bedroom.

I climbed back down the ladder and made my way over to my room, pushing open the secret doorway. Silence. No one was in there, not that I expected anyone to be.

It took all of ten minutes, but I packed up some clothes, my father's letters, and another pair of shoes in my backpack. With a sigh, I glanced back at the racks of clothes that I wouldn't see again. I knew it was too good to be true. That day shopping with Knight was like a dream ... but dreams were never real.

I left the room and tiptoed my way down the hall. Once I got to the stairs, I waited and listened. No sound. *Knight was probably fucking Kiki right now.* I sneered at the thought.

I crept down the stairs and glanced back one last time before slipping out the door. I kept to the edge of the property as I left. The last thing I wanted was for Knight to notice me walking away and come after me.

I thought about texting Arabella, but if the police wanted me, I wasn't about to get her in trouble for helping me hide.

It was a long shot, but there might be one place I could go. I opened my maps app and typed in the name. I groaned when I saw the distance. If I couldn't find a bus, it was going to be a long walk.

SIXTEEN

Knight

"SHE'S FUCKING GONE." I ran my fingers through my hair as I scanned the entranceway.

"Who's gone?" Arabella stood in her doorway with her arms crossed, looking very unhappy that I was in front of her.

"Violet. She's here, isn't she?" I stood on my tiptoes and tried to gaze past her.

"What? No, she's not here. And I haven't heard from her today. If you two had a fight, just walk it off, okay? Don't drag me into your twisted fantasies."

I lowered to my heels and tilted my head as I turned my gaze to her. "Fantasies? How would Violet leaving be a *fantasy*?"

She threw her arms up in the air. "I don't know. You two are always fighting about something. And then you're screwing. It doesn't take a rocket scientist to figure out you two get off on the push and pull stuff. It's your kink."

I narrowed my eyes at her. "I have no idea why Violet is friends with you."

"Because I care, that's why. I don't fuck with her like you do."

"I don't fuck with her . . .. Look, it

doesn't matter. We didn't have a fight. If you must know, I was keeping her in my attic due to—"

"What?" Her hands went up to stop me. "Do you hear yourself? You were keeping her in your attic. Like. A. Psycho." She pushed her finger into my chest.

I slapped her hand away.

"Is there somewhere a little more private we could talk?" I noticed some movement behind her.

Her gaze slid up and down my body as she pursed her lips. "Sure. Let's head to my car."

Was she about to drive me somewhere? Maybe to where Violet was hiding. I had texted and called Violet so many times in the last hour, and I felt like I was out of options. I went up to the attic once Kiki left, but Violet was gone. I noticed the letter and her backpack were gone too.

She had left in a hurry, and I worried someone had found her. Or maybe she was spooked by what her father wrote her, and she left on her own.

Whatever the reason, I needed to find her. If what Kiki told me was true, Violet was in danger.

I opened the passenger door to her car and slipped inside. Once Arabella was seated, she turned to me. "Okay, we can talk in here."

"You won't take me to her?"

"How should I know where she is? I already told you, I don't know."

My nose flared as I shook my head. "Seriously? She hasn't told you anything?"

Arabella shook her head.

"We haven't had a fight. Last I saw her, she was in the attic, where I had her hide because I knew the police would look for her. If they got a warrant to search my house, I wanted to make sure they didn't find her."

Arabella nodded. "I saw the news. She's the prime suspect for Crystal's murder. I understand why Violet might want to kill Crystal, but she isn't that sort of person. Someone who chopped up Crystal's body like that . . . that's a crazy person. Violet is the sanest person I know."

"Yeah, but that won't stop my uncle from trying to pin the murder on her, like he did for John Lenker. The police are also trying to pin the murder of the bus driver on her. But someone close to my uncle gave me evidence today of him admitting that Crystal killed the bus driver. They also gave me evidence that my uncle killed Crystal and John Lenker, along with some information to help me tie him to killing my parents and Jack Franklin."

Arabella's eyes widened. "Who is it?"

I knew Violet trusted Arabella, but I was too close to getting my uncle. It would only take one little slip for it all to crumble away.

"I can't tell you just yet, but the cards are stacked against my uncle. It won't be long before it all comes together."

"Thank God. That man needs to be locked up forever."

"Until then, Violet isn't safe. I need to make sure no one gets to her."

Arabella bit her lip, and it reminded me of Violet. My heart cracked. I never thought I would feel this way about anyone after my parents died. The anger and loss of it overwhelmed me.

I made a vow two years ago that I wouldn't let anything or anyone distract me from my purpose—to get my parents' killer. But once Violet stepped into my life, it became harder to focus on what was really important. Was it revenge that drove me, or love?

"Should we check her old trailer park?" Arabella asked.

I shook my head. "No, they have demolished it. Franklin First Laboratories is building a facility there."

My jaw tightened. I knew why the facility was being built—to make Elicit under the guise of an experimental cancer drug. My uncle covered his bases. No worry about importing the drugs illegally when he could just do it on American soil. The perfect plan for him—get rich while people got hooked.

And who was he hiring to work the lab? Violet's old neighbors and friends. They thought they were getting jobs. Little did they know they were contributing to ruining the lives of thousands.

"Oh yeah, I remember the mayor boasting about the job package he was implementing before he left office. I didn't realize the trailer park was the site for the new building."

"The only people who cared that the site was going to be that location were the people who lived there. And as far as my uncle was concerned, they weren't important. He despised them. He called them sad and was happy to wipe some of them off the map."

Wiping out where they lived or getting them hooked on a drug that would, at the very least, destroy their lives and, at most, would kill them, was a win-win to my uncle.

"I guess that's why he went after Violet," Arabella said with a sigh.

I twisted my lips. That was the one thing I couldn't figure out. I had my theories, but there wasn't any evidence why my uncle would want to hurt or kill Violet.

"I don't know. It must have something to do with her being Jack Franklin's daughter. But it's not as if he left her any money. She would have it by now if he did."

We both sat in the car wondering where to go. I grew anxious with every minute that ticked by.

"I wonder . . ." Arabella mumbled.

"Wonder what?"

She turned in her seat to face me. "There's a place Violet took me once, and I doubt your uncle would think to look for her there. It's a long shot, but we could try." Arabella didn't bother waiting for me to respond. She reached into a nook on the dashboard and pulled out a key.

Turning the car on, she said, "Buckle

up. I'm a lousy driver, which Violet has commented on several times."

I frowned and, just as I buckled my seatbelt, the car took off. My head hit the seat, and I realized Arabella wasn't joking.

I wasn't a praying person, but while in her car, I suddenly found God.

SEVENTEEN

Violet

THE DOOR TO THE office swung open and slammed against the wall, causing the framed pictures hanging there to shake.

I sat up and blinked at the tall woman standing in the doorway with a large stick in her hand.

"Here. Make yourself useful," Drew said as she pushed the broom at me.

I stood and came around the desk. "Yes. I'm happy to help."

When I ran from Knight's attic, Benny's Tattoo Parlor was the only place I could think of to go. Knight or his uncle would never find me here.

I grabbed the broom and glanced up at Drew. She stood with her arms folded, blocking the doorway.

"Do you want me to sweep in here?" I gazed about the room. There wasn't much floor for me to sweep as the room was smaller than the closet in my bedroom at Knight's house.

She jerked her head back. "Out there."

We stood and stared at each other.

"The only way I can sweep the floor out there is if you let me out."

Her eyes narrowed, and she leaned closer to my ear. "The only reason I'm letting you stay here is because Jewel told me to. Even if Jewel doesn't work here anymore, it doesn't mean she's not my friend."

I nodded. "I care about Jewel too—"

"You do? That's funny because the TV said you were wanted for her cousin's death. Killing someone's relative doesn't seem like a very *friendly* thing to do."

My lips thinned. I knew why she didn't trust me. But Drew never trusted me. If I was going to stay longer than a few hours, I had to get her to like me, or at least tolerate me.

"So all your friends who were wanted by the police, they were all guilty?"

She blinked, and her thin lips curved into a frown. "No, not all. Most of them were framed."

My brows shot up. "That happens. I should know. The mayor's framing me for a lot of things. And I had nothing to do with any of them."

Her head tilted. "The mayor? Our

mayor?"

"Yes, Mayor King."

Her expression went blank. I couldn't tell if she didn't want to deal with the headache of anything involving the mayor or if she just outright hated me.

"He destroyed my mom's trailer. She didn't get a cent for it. Just wiped out the trailer park and the nearby neighborhoods. All so he could build a lab."

I frowned. "I used to live there too."

I remembered the mayor telling me his big plans when I first arrived at his pool house—that terrible pool house where only horrific things occurred. All the money in the world wouldn't get me to step foot in that lavish place again.

"Even the townhouses were all torn down. It affected just about everyone on the south side. And where could we go? I was lucky. I lived in an apartment just outside of town, so my mom's staying with me. But others . . ." She shook her head. "That mayor is an asshole."

I smirked. "He's more than an asshole. He's a monster."

Her eyes slid down my body. "You used to live with him. Right?"

"Yes." My gaze fell to the floor. She probably hated me for it. I wouldn't be surprised if Drew thought I helped the mayor. Just by me being associated with him, most people assumed I liked him. That maybe I looked up to him.

"Did you know what he was planning?"

Shit. I sighed. It was better to be honest, no matter how much she'd hate me for it.

"He threatened me. Told me if I left or didn't do what he said, he'd hurt everyone I knew and loved. So, I did what he said. I never thought he'd go that far."

"So, you knew."

I glanced up into her cold, dark eyes. Her gaze never wavered.

I pushed my chin out. "Yes."

If she was going to kick me out, or worse, hit me, I'd deal with it. She had no idea what I dealt with because of the mayor. Drew had made up her mind about me long ago, so it didn't matter what I said.

Her eyes narrowed. "So what are you going to do about it?"

I blinked, unsure I heard her correctly. "What?"

"That man needs a beat down. If it were me, he'd already be on the ground crying for his mama. I'll ask again. What are you going to do about it?"

"I, uh—"

She took a step forward and pressed her finger into my shoulder, causing me to flinch. "You talk about being from the south side. Saying you lived in that trailer park, yet here you are, hiding from the world."

I swallowed. She was right. I ran from

Knight and from the mayor. It was time I stopped running and hiding. It was time for action.

"You're right." I twisted the tiny key on my bracelet. "If I ask for your help with something, would you be willing to—"

Her eyebrow rose. "Is it going to fuck with the mayor?"

"Absolutely."

She grabbed the broom from me and said, "Then I'm in."

EIGHTEEN

Violet

"**You wait in the** car. I'll be back." I leaned down once I stepped out of Drew's car before I shut the door and rested my elbow on the roof.

"How long is this going to take? Do I have time to grab a chocolate shake over at Bangers Burgers?" She pointed ahead.

I glanced down the darkening street. The sun was setting, and I needed to get into the building before it closed.

"I think so. I'll text you when I'm ready."

She held up her phone, and I told her my number. She texted me an okay emoji to let me know she had the right number. I slammed the door, and she drove off.

I sighed, wishing life was that easy. That I was spending my evening getting some fast food at Bangers Burgers instead of trying to track down my father's assistant, Janice Hartley, at Franklin First's primary office in downtown Green Hills.

I turned and stared up at the only building over five stories tall in the area. The windows looked black and sinister, and just being here had me on edge.

Taking a deep breath, I readied myself

for what awaited me inside. If anything.

I slid my hands into my coat pocket, and my fingers rubbed the edge of my dad's letter. Would Janice remember what my father told her? What if she didn't work there anymore?

"Fuck." I hadn't really thought that out.

I swallowed and made my way inside the building. The lobby was large with beige marble floors and walls with tall windows that looked out onto the street. Just behind the security desk sat a man who glanced up. His eyes scanned me as if he knew something dangerous might be hidden inside my coat.

My gaze shifted to the side of him where the elevators were in full view. I knew that look he gave me; no matter what I said to him, he wouldn't let me past.

I nibbled on my lower lip. Even if I got past him, where would I go? What floor?

My father died two years ago. I was doubtful there was any evidence left from when he was running the company. The closer I moved toward the guard's desk, the stupider I felt.

I rubbed my forehead as it hit me: that was why Knight took his time. He had a plan, and I had a very old letter. That was how he discovered the truth.

I glanced back toward the front door, through the glass walls. I noticed Drew's car wasn't out there. She hadn't come back yet.

I had two choices. Run out of here for fear of what that guard might do. Or I could face him and hope he took pity on the former owner's daughter.

Blowing out a loud breath, I shrugged. I had a pretty good idea which outcome was going to happen, but fuck it. I was tired of running.

"Can I help you?" The guard stood with his hands clasped in front of him like I was about to kick him in the junk. I would if he tried to grab me, but he didn't know that.

"I'm wondering if you could help me. I'm looking for a woman. I don't know if she still works here. She used to work with my father."

His eyes narrowed, and he pushed back the few brown strands on the top of his head. "I can't divulge who works here. I'm afraid—"

"Violet?" a woman's voice cut off the guard.

Both the guard and I turned our heads toward the elevator. Moving closer to me was a woman with shoulder-length black hair. Concern was etched into her features as her gaze flickered between me and the guard.

"Yes? Do I know you?"

"Violet Adler?" she asked as she stepped up to me, turning her back to the guard.

"Yes."

She gasped and threw her arms open. "I'm Janice Hartley. I used to be your father's assistant. He always kept a picture of you on his desk . . . that's how I recognized you."

My shoulders sagged. She did still work here. A wave of relief washed over me. I didn't have to deal with that guard who happened to still be giving me the stink eye.

Janice stepped forward and pulled me into a hug. My arms went around her. I didn't know her, but she knew my dad, and he trusted her, so I had a feeling she was on my side.

That was until she said something that made me regret ever stepping foot into the Franklin First building.

"No one here will help you. They are all out to get you," she whispered in my ear. "I suggest you come with me and not make a scene."

Janice pulled back; her dark eyes focused on me as a stiff smile formed on her lips. I tried to step back, but she grabbed my hand, her grip tight.

"Why don't we get something to eat? It's dinnertime. A growing girl like you must be hungry." Her grin fell. "I know just the place."

I looked over at the guard who was glaring at me, daring me to run.

The only person who could help me was in a car outside. Maybe Drew would notice Janice forcing me with her and follow us. I could wave at her car to signal her. Maybe even scream once we made it out of the building.

I tried to tug my arm back, but Janice wasn't having it. I sucked in a breath and focused on signaling Drew as Janice forced me to follow her out of the building.

For a second my heart raced as I saw a car pull up to the curb outside the building. The darkening evening sky made it hard to discern what type of car it was, but it had to be Drew.

As we stepped closer and I was about to raise my free hand to wave at the car, I noticed something off. The car was shiny, as if it had just been washed. And where there should have been a large dent on the side, it was perfectly smooth.

Someone stepped out, and it was a man, not Drew. I narrowed my eyes. The shape of the car was the same as Drew's, but as I got closer, I saw it was a completely unfamiliar car. The only similarities were the black color and that they both had four doors.

The back door opened, and Janice practically threw me inside. She was stronger than I thought.

"Where are we going?" I asked as I rubbed my arm.

Janice settled into her seat, and the door shut. She had her phone in her hand and was busy tapping at it. I glanced over and was about to lunge for the door on my side when she finally spoke.

"I wouldn't do that if I were you. Where will you run, Violet? Where can you go that we won't find you? Your father thought, with his money, he could do anything. Even knock up your whore of a mother and make believe he could have a happy little family with her. But the thing is, money can't buy everything. Not even loyalty." She smirked.

My heart pounded in my chest, but I

was more angry than scared. These people played games with lives. Not just life and death, but families ripped apart. And they laughed, only thinking of themselves.

The car moved, and I turned to face Janice, ready to wipe that smile off her face.

"So, you're loyal to a man who will kill you the moment you become irrelevant to him? He'll pin things on you that he did himself. And that's the best-case scenario. The worst . . ." I gritted my teeth at her, "you'll end up like my mom, at the bottom of a pond. Or like Crystal Hillingham, chopped up in a freezer."

I wasn't sure the mayor had anything to do with those murders, but based on what I understood about him and what had happened to my parents, I had a suspicion it was all Ichabod King's fault.

Janice's eyes flickered for a moment

with fear as my words broke through her icy wall. But within seconds, she was back to doing the mayor's bidding.

I glanced out the window as the car came to a stop.

"What are we doing at Jack's Place?"

What did the diner have to do with the mayor's plan?

A cheap diner that I still hadn't figured out why my father owned. Probably some nostalgic thing that a billionaire wanted to hold on to.

"You'll find out soon enough, Violet. Now get out."

What could I do? Refuse to get out until she forced me, only to get hurt in the process? I could take her on, but I'd still be wounded, and then how would I get away? I was sure her driver wouldn't let me get away from the person who signed his paycheck.

I was outnumbered, and there wasn't anyone who could help me. I sighed and opened the door.

When I stepped out, I gasped.

"What are you doing here?" I asked.

Kiki smiled. "Don't you know? Today's the day you get to be with your mother."

NINETEEN

Knight

"WHERE IS SHE?" I asked as I scanned the small tattoo parlor.

The woman's dark eyes narrowed as they slid up and down my body. I suspected she was buying time by the way she leaned against the broom handle.

"I see you made a mistake. This is a tattoo shop. You clearly want *Mind-Readers-R-Us*. They're down the block." She shook her head and mumbled the word "asshole" under her breath.

"Drew, right?" Arabella stepped out from behind me. "We're looking for Violet. I don't know if you remember me—"

"Yeah, I remember you, phone girl."

"Violet is my friend, and we're afraid she may be hurt. We just want to know where she is or if you have seen her?" Arabella asked with a stiff smile.

She was clearly uncomfortable. I suspected they had met before and didn't exactly get along.

"Yeah, I saw Violet. Tonight, actually. The funny thing is, she came to me for help. Not you. Why did she do that if you're her friends?"

I frowned. Violet and I had our difficulties, but I thought we were past that. After all I had done to help her, why didn't she trust me?

"I don't know." Arabella's eyes fell to the floor, and I got the sense that it hurt her. "It's mid-November. Two and a half months since I first met Violet. I've been there for her the entire time since she came to Green Hills Academy. Why wouldn't she come to me?"

Drew studied Arabella and sighed. "That is cold. And from what I know of Violet, she seemed like a nice person. Which is probably why I was so suspicious of her. It's always the nice ones who break your heart."

"Tell me about it." Arabella rolled her eyes. "That's why I don't date. Even the nice guys will dick you around. But I thought Violet . . . well, she's my friend."

"Maybe she was afraid you would get hurt?" Drew placed her broom against the wall. "She kept talking about fucking up the mayor. I got to wonder if he's going to hurt her too. Maybe she thought she was keeping you safe by trying to do it herself."

"Maybe . . ." Arabella said as she rubbed the back of her neck.

"She told you that?" I asked.

"She came here earlier. Wanted to hide out. Said where she was living, the guy had tricked her. Tried to lock her away, but she saw who he was meeting with, and it wasn't safe to be there either."

"Shit." I rubbed my face. "She saw me with Kiki."

Drew's eyebrows shot up. "You're the guy who locked her away?"

Arabella's eyes narrowed at me as Drew folded her arms over her chest. They both looked like they wanted to beat me down to the ground.

I held up my hands. "It was only so the police wouldn't find her. My uncle is the mayor—"

Within a second, Drew had grabbed the broom and held it like a bat. A bat she planned to use for batting practice with my head.

"Wait." I took a step back. "He killed my parents. I want to fuck up the mayor as much as Violet does. That's why I was hiding her. I know she didn't kill anyone. It was my uncle pinning those murders on her."

Arabella took a step closer to me. "Then why were you meeting with Kiki?"

"Because she's not who you think she is."

"The mayor's bimbo wife? I'm sure they don't have a perfect marriage, but I doubt she's about to cheat on him with his nephew." Arabella pushed her hands on her hips.

My gaze flickered between them both. There was no getting out of this without explaining everything.

For the next ten minutes, I told them everything that had happened to me over the past ten years. Even how I got the evidence that my uncle paid Jack Franklin's mechanic to cause the plane that held my parents and Violet's dad to crash in the Atlantic Ocean.

"But that still doesn't explain why you were talking to Kiki. Were you pretending to like her so she would spill some secrets?" Arabella asked.

Drew nodded. "Yeah, that's confusing. Why have anything to do with the mayor's wife?"

"Even if I hit on Kiki, it wouldn't matter. I am really not her type." My brows went up.

Arabella looked confused. "She doesn't like young guys? I thought for sure she'd be a total cougar. That bubble-gum-pink lipstick of hers was a complete giveaway."

"Maybe." I shrugged. "But I'm not the right sex for her."

I noticed the moment it registered with Arabella. Her eyes widened, and her mouth made an "O" shape.

"What? I had no idea. Then why is she married to the mayor?"

"Money," Drew and I said at the same time.

"Ewww." Arabella shuddered. "There's no amount of money I'd accept that would get me to marry his disgusting ass. No offense, Knight. I know he's your uncle, but he's a garbage person."

"I can't be offended when I totally agree with you. And now is the time to take out the trash."

"Right." Arabella turned to Drew. "So, do you know where Violet went?"

"We went downtown to the Franklin First building. I thought she would come out, but after an hour of waiting, I left. I tried texting her several times but got no response."

"So, she would still be in there if you never saw her leave," I commented.

"Uh, well . . . actually, I went to get something to eat when she first went in, but I came back. Waited for a while and then left. I had to get back to the shop." She waved around.

"My uncle knows people who work there. I hope they didn't get to her. Let's head over there to find out what happened. Thanks, Drew." I nodded to her.

"Oh, I'm coming. If the mayor is as bad as you told me, then I'd be happy to give him a beat down."

"Let me call for backup too. The more people we have with us, the better chance we have at making sure Violet is safe."

I texted Briggs and Caleb to meet us downtown at the Franklin First building. I was about to put my phone in my pocket when an idea popped in my head. I texted one more person and hoped they got it in time.

The hairs on the back of my neck stood on end as I got into Arabella's car. I had a bad feeling we might be too late.

TWENTY

Violet

THE SKY WAS ALREADY an inky black, and I noticed there were only two other cars in the parking lot. I swallowed as Janice's fingers dug into my arm as she pushed me toward the diner door.

"I hope we're ordering food because I

haven't had dinner," I said as Kiki reached for the door and opened it.

"You're a little smartass just like your dad. God, how I hated working for him."

A metallic scent made me frown when the door opened. Janice shoved me inside, and I stumbled, ultimately falling to the floor.

I fell into a puddle, something thick and wet. I lifted my hand, believing at first it was a melted milkshake. But when I saw the deep red color, I screamed. Scrambling back, I bumped into someone.

Glancing up, a man stood over me, smiling. The same sickening grin I had learned to despise.

"Hello, little girl. You lost?" the mayor asked in a way that I suspected he wasn't expecting an answer.

"The stupid bitch walked right into Franklin First. We didn't even need to lure her there. Looks like this will be easier than we thought," Janice said as she came near.

I tried to get up, but my legs wobbled and I kept slipping on the blood.

But whose blood was it?

"Ugh, Ichabod. Now we have to clean this up?" Kiki said as she waved at the floor.

The mayor's gray eyes flickered up to his wife. A smile curved the corner of his mouth. "Do we? I think we will leave things exactly the way they are."

All three of them stood around me, caging me in. Even if I could stand, I felt safer down on the floor.

My stomach rolled as I tried my best to swallow the bile rising in my throat. I tried to scoot farther from the blood, but they wouldn't let me.

"Please, I need to use the bathroom," I said between gasps.

Don't puke, Violet.

"If you're going to retch, do it here. It just adds to the evidence," the mayor said.

"Evidence?" Kiki asked.

"Jesus Christ, Kiki. The bodies." He waved a hand across the diner.

The women stepped aside, and I finally saw where all the blood was coming from. There, on the floor, was a woman. It was the server who gave me the envelope from my father.

Seraphina sat in a booth near the body, but she looked different. I gasped when I realized why. She had been shot in the head. Her body was propped up by the booth as her head slumped forward.

"I'm pinning this all on Violet. Haven't you figured it out by now?" the mayor said and then waved his hand at her as if dismissing her. "You always were an idiot. Honestly, Janice, I don't know what you see in her."

Janice raised a brow. "You haven't seen her naked."

Both Janice and Ichabod laughed while Kiki huffed and went over to a booth far from the bodies.

With Kiki out of the way and feeling coming back to my legs, I took another chance and stood. But when I did, I must have done it too fast as there was no stopping the puke from coming up. I bent over and retched.

"There we go. Now I can say that Seraphina confronted you with the murder of her mom. You shot her, and when the waitress tried to stop you, you killed her too. Once you realized what you did, you became ill. It's more believable that way." The mayor nudged me with his elbow.

"You're sick." I shook my head and wiped my mouth on my sleeve, the one not covered in blood.

"No, little girl, I'm rich. And once you are dead, I will take over Franklin First and become the wealthiest person in the United States. Even your sweetheart Knight can't stop me."

An icy chill ran down my spine. This

was it. The night I died. Murdered. Just like my parents. Or were they . . .? I never discovered that.

"Did you kill them?"

He waved at the bodies and laughed. "Of course I did."

"No, my parents. Did you kill my mom and dad?"

The mayor rolled his eyes, strolled over to the booth next to Kiki and sat. "Since you're about to die, I might as well tell you the truth. Your dad and I were friends growing up. But after college, he suddenly cleaned up his act. Didn't want to rub elbows with me anymore. No more getting girls drunk at the clubs and then banging them. He turned into a bore."

I frowned at the thought of what he was like when he was young.

"Your dad used to be cool. Then he met your mom, and suddenly, he wanted to be a family man. But he was my friend, and your mom didn't like me very much.

Especially when I cornered her in the bathroom at Jack's house. Fucking bitch kneed me in the crotch."

Way to go, Mom. I wanted to shout it, but I stayed silent. It was more important to hear the truth.

"When Jack found out, he never wanted to speak to me again. Well, that's just not done in our circles. So, I told his family, who quickly made sure he dumped your mom. But the asshole kept seeing her—only because she trapped him by getting pregnant. She thought she could get his money by getting knocked up. That bitch had it coming."

"That bitch was my mom," I ground out through gritted teeth.

"Exactly. So, I played the long game. That's what smart people do. Once you were born, I leaked information to Jack about your mom. Things that weren't true, of course. But slowly, he believed. The thing is, you tell a lie enough, people believe it."

"Asshole." I clenched my fists but stayed still. If he was going to kill me tonight, I was going down with a fight. And I fought dirty with my nails.

He threw his hand back and laughed. "God, I know. I'm the worst. But the best part were the letters I sent to both of them. In each, I claimed to be the other person. Do you know that's how I got your mom hooked on drugs? I sent her *vitamins*. I made it look like Jack swore they would help her health. Since Jack owned a pharmaceutical company, she believed the letter and started taking the vitamins."

He leaned over the table toward Kiki. "They weren't vitamins. They were addictive drugs."

"Wasn't it enough that they were apart? That my mother and I barely scraped by. You had to get her hooked, too? You vengeful son of a bitch." Tears streamed down my face as the hell that was my life was told by a guy who thought it was like playing a board game. I was just another game piece for him to knock over.

He leaned forward, his eyes darkening. "No. You don't fuck with me. You don't say no to me. I decided the only way to get back at Jack and your mom was to destroy them. Oh, and get rich in the process. When I saw what that failed cancer drug was doing to the testers, I knew I had gold on my hand. Jack had to die. But then you were in the way."

I shook my head. "How was I in the way? I was living on the south side with a drug-addicted mom. Hardly your competition."

He reached into his jacket pocket and took out a piece of paper. "This is the will I thought your father left. But, as his lawyer pointed out, it's not the most recent version. He remembers drawing up a new will, which your father insisted be handwritten because he wanted no electronic record of it. That asshole. But then he hid it here, according to Janice."

The mayor sighed as if this was boring him before he continued, "Your father left you everything. His estates, his cars, Franklin First, and even this shitty diner. But for the life of me, I can't open the safe. Trust me, I tried. I know the will is in the safe in that office back there."

I turned my head and glanced back. The room where the waitress gave me the letter.

I turned back to face him. "How would I know anything about that?"

"That waitress told me Jack left you a letter. It must hold a combination and a key." Ichabod strummed his fingers on the table.

The paper with those numbers. My eyes dipped to my jacket pocket. I had brought the letter with me, including the page with the numbers.

"Get her," the mayor said.

Janice was on me before I could dash away, her hands plunging into my pockets. I tried to pull her hands out, but it was no use.

I gave up on trying to get her out of my pockets and used my nails. My fingers went up to her face, and I clawed her like a good south-sider would.

"You fucking cunt." Janice tried to shake me off her, but it was no use. There was blood on her face, but I had no idea if it was hers or what I had smeared on my hands from the floor.

"I got it." She pulled away, breathless, holding up the pages.

I lunged for her, but the mayor stood and plucked the papers from Janice's hands. Glancing over at Kiki, I saw her checking something on her phone. I guess fighting for my life was boring for her. Plastic bitch.

The mayor flipped through the papers, and I saw his eyes light up as they found the paper with all the numbers.

"Great. We got the combination. Now all we need is the key." He gazed over at me.

I shook my head. "I never got a key. My father just left me those letters, nothing more."

"You're lying to me. Let me put it this way to you, little girl." He reached into his jacket and pulled out a gun.

I swallowed as my eyes focused on the black metal.

"I can make your death quick, or I can make it excruciatingly long and painful, much like I did your mom when I drowned her at Happy Pond."

My face scrunched up in pain. The thought of her suffering as she died ripped me in two. A sob tore out of my throat.

"That's right. It was me. She was supposed to meet someone to get a passport for you both. Trying to run off to Canada or some shit. She found out some things about me, and the woman was smart enough to run and take you with her. But I was smarter. I met her there and dragged her to the middle of the pond and pushed her down until she drowned. I was going to do the same thing to you, but my stupid nephew showed up."

Knight really saved me.

"Your mom pleaded for your life. Told me you knew nothing. That she even gave you some sleeping medicine to whisk you away because she knew you would fight leaving and ask too many questions. I didn't believe her." He shrugged. "But it turned out, she was right. You were just a stupid little girl."

My legs shook, and I worried I'd pass out. That was why my mom drugged me. Not because she was on some crazy bender; no, she wanted to save me. She knew I was stubborn enough to fight her. Fuck.

And now she was gone. *I'm so sorry,*

Mom. I'm so sorry for everything.

"Now give me that key." There was a click of the gun, and I flinched. I thought he was about to shoot, but he did it only to scare me.

But I couldn't give him what I didn't have. I smiled at that. No matter what happened, I'd die tonight. But he wouldn't get what he wanted.

"And what are you going to do with that will?"

"Make adjustments. Have me as the beneficiary of Franklin First. I don't want his other money. I have my own property, but his company. . . that's where the actual money and power lie. Once I have the shackles of the mayorship off my neck, I can really do what I want. Manufacture those addictive little pills in the new south side factory and get so many people hooked . . . I'll make billions for the rest of my life."

"And we'll be rich too," Janice said.

The mayor's smile faded. I suspected he didn't like other people taking the money. Janice didn't have long herself.

"And you think what happened to Crystal or Seraphina won't happen to you?" I pointed at the woman who brought me here.

Her smirk turned to a frown as my words made sense once again. But right before she was about to say something, there was a noise at the front door.

It opened, and Knight walked inside.

"What's a guy got to do to get some service around here?" he said with a chuckle.

I shook my head. No, no, he shouldn't have been here. The mayor would kill him too.

"This night just keeps getting better and better," the mayor said, raising his gun and pointing it at Knight.

TWENTY-ONE

Violet

KNIGHT'S EYES SWEPT THE room, and the moment he saw the bodies, he grew pale.

"Come in, my dear nephew, join the party," Ichabod said as he jerked the gun.

Knight took a deep breath, and as he let

it out, he straightened. He took a few steps and hopped over the blood. He came to my side and whispered, "Are you okay?"

"As okay as I can be having fell into their blood." I held up my hands.

His eyes searched my hands. "I'm glad it's not your blood. Don't worry, we'll get out of this."

I swallowed. I had been doubting Knight for too long. All this time it had been his uncle, and I was too wrapped in my head to realize it. The doubt I had for my father and for my mother was the same doubt I had for Knight.

It was time for me to trust him. To learn to trust people who wanted to help me. Even if I couldn't see what he could do to get us out of this mess, I would put my faith in him.

"I love you," I said as I stared up into his sparkling gray eyes. The more I searched them, the more I realized his eyes were nothing like his uncle's.

Knight's eyes held hope and heart. His uncle's heart died long ago, if he ever had one.

His nostrils flared, and he placed his hands on my arms. He was about to say something when the mayor interrupted.

"Oh, look at that. The two love birds saying their goodbyes to each other."

Knight smirked but continued to look down at me. "I know what you did, Uncle. All those lives you took. You were the one who paid the mechanic and caused my parents to die."

"Uh, that was a mistake. I will be the first to admit it." The mayor tilted his head as if he was trying to remember something. "I really only wanted Jack Franklin dead, not your parents. I mean, that's my brother. It's not like I'm a monster," he said with a snort.

Knight turned and took a step forward, but his uncle stopped him by waving the gun at him.

"And yet, you showed no remorse for what you did. Accident or not, you still purposely killed Violet's dad."

"What's done is done. So I had to break a few eggs to get what I wanted. Don't you see? I have it now. Well, once she's dead." He waved the gun toward me. "I have the drug and will own the company that makes it. I have the connections. And, as a former mayor, once the new mayor is sworn in come January, I will have the clout with nothing holding me back."

"Like laws," I spat out.

"You call them laws, but they don't apply to people like me—the ones with power and money. We don't get arrested. And even if I did, the most I'd get would be a few months in jail. What's that? It's nothing. Because once I got out, I'd still have all my money."

"What about John Lenker? You killed your friend?" Knight asked.

"He was getting scared because you

filmed him trying to fuck your girlfriend. What was I going to do? He had to go. And as for Crystal . . . she screwed it all up when she killed that bus driver. Suddenly there was attention on that, and I couldn't have it. Her stupid daughter," he waved his gun toward Seraphina's body, "tried to threaten me. She told me she was going to the police about how I killed her mom. She's as stupid as her mom."

"But I saw you leave the Pumpkin Luncheon. Crystal was still in the basement at that point."

His uncle raised his brow. "I'm the mayor. Of course they let me in when I came back mentioning I left something in the basement. And did anyone bat an eye when I lugged out a huge rolled up rug? Kiki helped, of course, being the dutiful wife."

"You racked up quite a kill list."

The mayor was about to say something, but suddenly we heard the door to the diner close. Everyone turned to look, and we realized Kiki had left.

Janice went to the door and opened it. "She's run off."

"Let her. I'll deal with her later. It's not like she can do any harm now."

"You sure about that, Uncle?" Knight rubbed his chin.

The mayor narrowed his eyes at his nephew. What was Knight talking about? My gaze flickered between them, and the memory of Knight meeting with Kiki popped into my head.

That felt like a lifetime ago, but it was only earlier today. Did Kiki let Knight know what was going down with his uncle?

Maybe Knight wasn't cheating on me but getting information on Ichabod.

"What are you talking about? She's my wife."

Knight shook his head as he chuckled. "Come off it. We all know your marriage is a sham. Janice is the one banging her, not you."

"Your attempt to anger me isn't really working, Knight. It's not like the public will find out. And I'm really tired of playing this game with you. I think it's time to stop this." The mayor stood and took a few steps closer.

"Who to kill first . . ." He bounced the gun between both of us. "The asshole nephew who couldn't leave well enough alone? Or the trash-heap bitch who was stupid enough to stick around, even when I warned her that I was going to destroy her?"

I winced as it reminded me about the note in my locker on the first day. Every horrible thing that had happened in my life, from my mom becoming addicted to drugs to never knowing my dad to the torment I received when I came to the north side was because of one man.

Ichabod King.

The muscles in my chin flexed as I

ground my teeth. I took a step forward and said, "Is that all you got, shithead? You're such a coward. Hiding behind others to gain power and money. It's always someone else who did all the hard work, and then you stole it. Took all the credit. The drug. The money. You can't even get a wife to like you. You're a loser, and even that gun won't get that stink off you."

If I was going to die, then he needed to hear the truth.

His tongue slid across the front of his teeth. "Fine. It looks like you get to watch your boyfriend die."

The mayor lifted the gun, and then Knight said, "Make sure when you kill me, you smile. Wouldn't want the people on the internet not see those gleaming white teeth of yours as you pull the trigger."

The mayor hesitated. His eyes frantically searched the room. Janice slipped out the door, which closed with a bang, and the mayor stared at it with an open mouth.

"Oh, don't worry. The cops will deal with her later too." Knight threw his thumb over his shoulder.

"You're lying." The mayor raised his gun again, but his eyes kept flicking from left to right.

"No. Unlike you, I don't like to lie."

I could hear sirens in the distance. The mayor turned toward the door, and it worried me that he would run. But right at that moment, the front door opened, and in walked Briggs and Caleb.

Knight stepped forward and snatched the gun out of his uncle's hand. "I'll take this. You might as well have a seat, Mayor. You aren't going anywhere."

The police arrived within a few minutes, and once they did, a few people came out from the back hallway. That journalist I remembered when I arrived at the pool house on the first day, Arabella, and Drew.

I ran over and gave Arabella a hug. We all turned to watch as the mayor was dragged out in handcuffs, looking utterly deflated. I didn't think I had ever witnessed a more satisfying moment in my life.

"What was Knight talking about, smiling for the camera?" I asked the others as Knight spoke to an officer.

"That would be me." The journalist waved her phone in the air. "Hi, I'm Georgia Ellis. I was hiding in the kitchen and was live streaming the event. I have about ten thousand followers on my channel, and they got notifications about what was happening. At this moment, this video was my most watched one of the day. And the comments." She whistled. "Let's just say, they're calling for justice—and not in the nicest way."

"Thank you, Ms. Ellis." I was about to clasp her hand in mine but remembered the blood.

"Please, call me Georgia."

"Oh God, is that Seraphina?" Arabella asked as she covered her mouth with her hand.

I never liked Seraphina, but I would never wish her to be murdered.

"Yes. Let's hope the mayor goes away for a long time after what he did."

They all told me how Drew helped track me down by threatening to beat up the security guard at Franklin First. That Knight had met with Kiki because she worried the mayor would kill her too, especially after what happened to Crystal. She gave Knight a bunch of evidence—all the missing pieces.

I told them I would explain what I knew, but first, I wanted to wash my hands. I went into the bathroom and looked at myself in the mirror. There was blood smeared on my cheek.

Blinking at what I saw, it all sank in. A lifetime of heartache and pain was now over. No more worrying that someone was out to get me or wondering who my father was.

No more anger for my mom. The moment the mayor lost was the moment I got the life I never knew I had.

The tears fell as I washed away the blood. I did my best and looked forward to getting home and stepping into a hot shower. I would scrub my body until I turned into a prune.

I wondered if Knight still wanted me to live at his place? I guessed it wasn't necessary anymore. Perhaps I could stay with Arabella for a little while until my aunt found an apartment.

There was a knock at the bathroom door. I went over and opened it. Knight leaned against the frame, his eyes roaming my face. He looked tired but at peace.

"How are you holding up?" he asked in the gentlest voice.

"As well as I can for someone who was

almost killed and had a *Carrie* prom moment." I held out my shirt, still soaked in blood.

"Come here." He pulled me close and wrapped his arms around me. It felt good to be held. I relished the feeling of his powerful arms and the warmth of his body.

"It's over," I mumbled into his shirt.

I inhaled, filling my lungs with his scent. I thought about all we had been through together. There was no other person I wanted to hold me right now. He understood more than anyone what hell was like. We walked those uneasy, burning coals together. There were many times I thought he was the devil, but I realized, he was my savior.

"It is. Yet, the pain hasn't disappeared," he said.

I took a shuddering breath. "I know. I don't think it ever will, but at least there will be justice."

"Yes. There's no way my uncle will get out of this."

We stood there holding each other and digesting the events of the evening. After what felt like seconds but was more like several minutes, Knight pulled back and said, "Why don't we find that will?"

I blinked. "But I don't have the key."

He reached for my hand and lifted it, turning over my wrist as he pointed at the bracelet my father had left me. "Yes, you do."

My eyes widened. "Holy shit. That's what the bracelet is. The key to his safe."

TWENTY-TWO

Violet

One Month Later

"I NEVER REALIZED THE Holiday Dance was held in the school gym. As fancy as Green Hills Academy is, I expected it would be in a ballroom on some grand estate." I gazed at the twinkling lights that were strung over the beams in the ceiling.

"The dance committee wanted to slum it this year." Knight's lips curled into his usual devilish grin. "The past few years they held it at the Hillingham's, but with all that happened, they decided against it." Knight slipped his arm in mine.

Once the mayor was arrested, the entire Hillingham home was searched because of his connection to Crystal's murder and Seraphina's body at the diner. The video of the mayor almost raping me was found. They used it as evidence against the mayor, though my face was blurred out when it was played in court. Pieces of it got out, but because no one knew who the girl in the video was, they assumed it was Seraphina—especially since she was the one who had the video on her computer.

Part of me was glad everyone knew what a monster the mayor was, but the other part of me hated seeing that video.

"Thanks for being my date. I don't think I've ever had a date to a dance. I usually just went with my girlfriends, if I went at all."

My eyes slid down his body. He wore a dark suit and tie, and he wore it well. I felt my body flush. He slid his fingers over mine, and I reacted just the same as the first time he touched me. I wondered if my body would ever stop reacting to his.

"I should be the one thanking you. I was supposed to go with Seraphina." He frowned, remembering her fate. "I still have trouble getting what happened to her out of my head."

I pulled back. "I know. It was awful, but I had no idea you planned to go to the dance with her. You told me you two broke up back in the early summer."

Knight pulled me along with him as we

made our way over to the table with refreshments. I thought he wouldn't answer me as he lifted a crystal glass filled with red punch to me. I clasped it and brought it to my lips.

It was good. Refreshing and had a fruity taste with a hint of citrus to it. He took a glass for himself, but before he took a sip, Knight said, "I had made a deal with her at the end of the summer. She kept begging me back, and I finally promised her one date to the Holiday Dance if she would help me get the deed to my house transferred over to my name. I didn't want to take a chance that my uncle would get the property."

"Didn't your parents leave it to you in their will?"

"Yes, but you know my uncle . . .."

My brow arched. "Thankfully not anymore." I gave a wide smile.

Knight studied my teeth. "New tooth looks good."

I slid my tongue around the new dental implant. After all that happened last month with the mayor at Jack's Place, I finally had time to get my tooth fixed.

They arrested Janice with the charge of stealing drug information from Franklin First. Knight's uncle was awaiting trial for murder and distribution of an illegal substance. He had been nicknamed the Murdering Mayor for all the bodies that came from his hands.

As for Kiki, she was cooperating with the FBI to get a reduced sentence for participation in creating the drug Elicit and helping remove Crystal's body from the basement of the Hillingham home.

"Let's toast." Knight raised his glass. "To a new tooth and getting into Winter River University. No more thoughts of my uncle and all involved in it."

"You got in too?"

Just over two months ago I was accepted to apply. I thought that was the best moment of my life, but that changed yesterday when I got my acceptance letter. I was so busy filling out paperwork with the Franklin First lawyers that needed to be completed for me to formally become head of the company. In title only . . . for now.

"I am a King," Knight said with a smirk.

We both took a sip.

"Oh my god, Violet, I love your dress," Arabella said as she showed up at my side.

I bit my lip and pulled out the skirt, swaying it back and forth. "Thanks, it's my very first indulgence."

Knight and I found the safe in my father's office at the diner. With the combination and the key on my bracelet, it opened right up. Inside were letters, supposedly from my mom.

I read them all and knew they were the forgeries the mayor had spoken of. There was no way my mom would have written those things; besides, it didn't even look like her handwriting.

The last envelope contained my father's will, dated two days before his death. In it, he left me everything. I now had a home—rather, many homes—of my own.

My aunt nearly fainted when I told her how much I was worth. I told her to quit her job because I would take care of her, and she didn't hesitate. No more travel for her.

And I discovered why my dad owned that diner. It was the one place he and my mom could meet that no one knew about. She used to take me there when I was little.

I didn't remember, but I suspect that was why it always felt comforting. I had been there, but the memories had faded. But once my mom was hooked on drugs, she didn't want him to see her like that, so she stopped taking me.

"I went shopping a few days ago and got it. What do you think?"

"It's gorgeous. But I'm kind of mad you didn't take me with you." Arabella frowned.

"I'll take you with me when I go car shopping tomorrow."

"Finally. I don't have to chauffeur you around anymore," she said with a dramatic sigh.

"Whatever, you'll miss me." I glanced around. "Who's your date?"

"Dates. Plural." She winked and pointed to three guys standing near the bleachers. "I'm going to have so much fun tonight. Wait a second." She lifted onto her tiptoes. "Is that the new girl?"

I glanced around and ended up on my tiptoes as well. "Oh my god, you're right."

"I wonder who she came with." Arabella wiggled her eyebrows.

She knew something. That girl knew everything about everyone. I was about to lean in to ask her to spill it when I felt a tug on my arm.

Knight leaned in and whispered in my ear, "I have something to show you."

His hot breath tickled my neck, and I felt my nipples harden.

"Okay." I turned to Arabella and explained I'd be right back.

Knight guided me toward the boys' locker room. Both Briggs and Caleb were inside. Knight nodded to them, and they nodded back.

"Is this where the secret nodding

society meets?" I asked with a snort.

"Such a smartass." Knight slapped my ass cheek and sent a wave of heat between my thighs.

"Have fun, you two," Briggs said with a snicker before they both left the room.

"Seriously, what's happening?"

"I have a gift for you." He walked over to his locker and opened it up. Knight pulled out a small box wrapped in white paper with a blue bow.

He held it up and said, "The police finally released this because of some pressuring from me." He pushed it toward me.

I grabbed it, confused as to what it could be.

After I unwrapped it, I saw it was a large jewelry box. Something that would hold a bracelet or necklace. When I lifted the lid, I lost my breath.

My hand flew to my chest as I gasped. I could barely believe what I was seeing.

"How did you—" My voice failed me as I choked on my words.

He lifted the necklace and held it up. "The police were holding it as evidence, but it was boxed up and forgotten. I demanded to see all the evidence they had on your mom, and I saw this inside. I thought you might want it."

"It's my mom's locket. She always wore it. My baby picture's inside." I plucked it from his hand and opened the locket. The picture was more faded than I realized, but you could tell it was a baby picture.

"No, it's not."

"What?" I tilted my head.

"It's not a baby picture of you. The police did their research. That is a picture of your dad as a baby."

I gasped and studied the small

photograph. "So, I had a picture of him my entire life, just hanging from my mom's neck. Why would she keep a baby—" I stopped as it hit me.

This was the only way she could keep him next to her heart. If it had been an adult photograph of him, anyone who got a hold of the necklace might figure it all out. This way, only she would know.

A lone tear drifted down my cheek. "I always thought it was me . . .."

His thumb went up to my face, wiping away the tear.

"I love you, Violet. While our parents can't be here to help you, know that I won't let anything bad happen to you again."

I gazed up into his mesmerizing gray eyes and smiled. "And I'll keep the sass coming."

"You better." He reached around and grabbed my ass, giving it a firm squeeze.

THE END

About the Author

Josie Max is the second pen name for a USA Today Bestselling author. She's a passionate writer of dark heroes, twisted tales, and delicious love stories. Her other passions include reading and coffee. Obviously, she has no life. But that's good, because more time to think up wicked, dark romances with bullying men and fierce heroines. When she's not writing, she's rangling her two little boys and snuggling up with her husband at night so they can pass out from exhaustion together after putting the kids to bed.

www.josiemaxwrites.com